BEDROOM EYES

Becky Barker

A KISMET® Romance

METEOR PUBLISHING CORPORATION
Bensalem, Pennsylvania

To Kathy Holland, my best friend and soulmate, who waited more than ten years for "the rest of this story."

And always, for my guy with the bedroom eyes.

BECKY BARKER

Becky Barker lives in Ohio with her husband, Buzz, and their three teenagers: Rachel, Amanda, and Thad. She's an avid reader of romances and considers herself one of those lucky people whose life has been filled with music, laughter, and love. She enjoys hearing from readers and can be reached by writing: P.O. Box 113, Mt. Sterling, Ohio 43143

Other books by Becky Barker:

ONE

Liana stretched one long, shapely leg out the bedroom window, and then the other. Her bare feet found footholds on an old trellis, and she eased herself carefully down the side of the house. The brief physical exertion brought out a sweat that made her skimpy clothing cling to her damp flesh. It was only six A.M. and she was already hot, tired, and irritable.

Mere seconds after her feet touched ground, she was joined by an aging but aggressive Pekingese who still managed to stir up more trouble than a whole litter of puppies.

"If you plan to go with me, then plan to behave yourself," she admonished in a whisper.

Smokey responded with an unblinking stare from beady eyes and an energetic wagging of his tail. He looked ready for action, and Liana frowned at the idea. The Peke followed closely as she walked from the big, white farmhouse that had belonged to her family for more than a century.

7

They passed the barn without attracting attention and then moved slowly through the dairy herd's grazing pasture. Once they had crossed the western corner of her dad's farm toward his farthest boundary fence, they would be nearing Liana's favorite hideaway.

She forced herself to relax and enjoy the freshness of the country morning. The grass was high and thick, deeply green and covered with dew. Turtle doves cooed a love song while the rooster crowed his superiority from the hen house. The scent of freshly mown alfalfa hay hung sweetly in the morning haze, and Liana inhaled deeply. She'd forgotten how much she loved the smell.

"I've been away an awfully long time, haven't I?" she asked her miniature sidekick.

Three sharp barks and some frantic prancing answered the question. Then Smokey dashed under the white board fence that separated her dad's land from land belonging to the Drenasis estate. He wiggled beneath the bottom rung as Liana swung to the top, straddling the rail while hungrily surveying the tranquil sight before her.

The pond was the size of a football field, and was continually flushed by an artesian spring. It had always been a private playground for Liana.

Poor Mr. Drenasis had lived the life of a recluse until she'd befriended him at the age of twelve. She'd been allowed the run of his mansion home and spent hours listening to tales of his Greek homeland. He'd died last year without any known heirs. Liana felt a twinge of guilt for having been too busy to come home for the funeral.

His fabulous home and thirty-five-hundred-acre farm had sold at a sheriff's auction to some business tycoon from New York. She supposed that technically she was trespassing, yet she didn't hesitate to jump the fence. She doubted that the new owner would ever set foot on this section of land. If he'd bought the place as an investment, he probably wouldn't care about the unproductive and isolated portion of his property.

This place was as much a part of Liana's life as her own backyard. The sparkling pool with its halo of willow trees held special memories. She moved toward the pond and seated herself on a large, flat stone facing the water.

Smokey dropped at her feet, apparently exhausted, but she doubted his inactivity would last. He was getting old, yet he had a youthful penchant for mischief, and she adored him even if he was a nuisance.

The sun penetrated the thick morning haze and shone like a golden arrow piercing the sky, striking the water with a shaft of brilliance. The temperature was already in the mid-eighties, and the humidity soared even higher. Central Ohio was having an unusually hot springtime this year.

The atmosphere seemed more stifling after her walk, and Liana fretfully tugged at her cotton top. There wasn't a puff of air to stir the breeze, yet the gentle gurgling of the water echoed in the stillness of the morning. The sound was a tantalizing invitation for Liana to cool her fevered limbs in the pond's refreshing depths.

She'd always followed the rule about not swimming alone. Her parents would be alarmed if they knew she'd come this far, and they'd be appalled at the thought of her exerting enough energy to swim.

"What the hell?" she groused, giving Smokey her

undivided attention for an instant. "I'm not an invalid."

Smokey snorted, and so did Liana. The water gently mocked her inhibitions. Its cooling depths taunted and coaxed. It was a delightful temptation that she had little will to resist. She slid to the ground, stepped out of her shorts, and pulled off her top. Then her fingers bravely unfastened the hooks of her bra, tossing it to the flat rock where she'd been sitting. Defiance waned somewhat as she considered removing her bikini briefs.

"Modesty," she explained out loud.

With a tinkling laugh closely followed by a sigh of self-indulgence, Liana slid her overheated body into the coolness of the pond. The caressive rippling of water against her bare skin sent tiny shivers of awareness to every nerve ending, and she gasped when the tingling sensations flowed over her.

Due to the constant churning of the artesian spring, the water was cool and lapped against her flesh with a rhythmic motion that was totally erotic. Liana closed her eyes and savored the feel. She badly needed relief from the physical tension and emotional strain of the past few months.

She'd been such a fool. She'd been too impatient, too ambitious, too careless with her health. After cramming four years of college study into three years, she'd set out to make a name for herself in New York. She'd worked sixteen-hour days and pushed herself to the limit until she'd landed in the hospital with pneumonia complicated by mononucleosis.

The doctors told her if she didn't take care of herself, she'd irreparably damage her lungs and liver.

Her parents had been frantic, and she'd rashly promised to move home with them for the entire summer.

"The fever must have cooked my brain," she murmured as she began to swim across the pool with sure strokes and natural grace.

She felt stronger every day. She wanted to get back to work, and the inactivity was driving her nuts. If only Rod were home, she thought wistfully. He was due back any day now. She wouldn't feel so bereft once he was here.

Rodney Govern was the tall, dark, handsome man of her dreams. She'd loved him for as many years as she'd known him, and that was all her life. He was two years older than she and had attended an out-of-state college while she'd commuted to Ohio State University.

Their time together had been limited. He'd spent the last five years globe-hopping from one engineering project to another while she'd devoted her every waking breath to a career in interior design.

Rod would be home from South America soon, and they could discuss the future. They hadn't spoken of marriage lately, but it had been a shared dream to one day marry and raise a family.

Liana slowly swam back and forth across the pond, utilizing every swimming stroke she'd ever learned. She was regaining her strength, and it felt marvelous. From now on she intended to guard her health.

Gradually, prompted by a childish urge to disrupt the pond's tranquillity, Liana began to play more energetically. She dove to the bottom and skimmed the water's depth until she was forced to surface for air.

Then she splashed and kicked to see the spray sparkle in the sunlight with prismatic glory. Standing on tiptoe, her waist-length hair cloaking her nudity, she threw handfuls of water at the sun and laughed delightedly as it showered back down on her up-turned face.

A contented smile transformed earlier weariness to loveliness when she eventually allowed the pool to return to its peaceful state. Now she would float lazily on her back. She felt vitally alive and totally sensuous as the sun's rays bathed her naked breasts with erotic heat.

She considered the fact that her restlessness might be due to unsatisfied physical and emotional needs. Her discontent might be attributed to more than a lengthy recovery and the curtailing of her career. Maybe the summer would bring an end to the restless yearnings, she mused dreamily while an unusual stillness settled around the pond.

Suddenly, inexplicably, Liana's serenity was shattered by an intense feeling of vulnerability. Her feet dropped to the pool bottom, and her head shot up proudly, blue eyes searching for the cause of her unease.

Her senses were highly attuned to her surroundings and alerted to danger. Her glittering gaze scanned the embankment until lighting on the cause of her sensual alarm. A tall, tanned, blond man leaned non-chalantly against the boulder where she'd been sitting earlier.

Disturbingly masculine and potentially dangerous, he returned her shocked glance with bold disregard for her privacy. His arms were crossed over his chest and he appeared relaxed, but Liana had the impression he was patiently waiting for her to make one wrong move.

He was Rod's size, six feet tall and muscular, but from her angle, he took on the dimensions of a giant. His brazen eyes remained glued to her, and she felt hot color scorching its way over her neck to her cheeks.

Never having found herself in such an outrageous situation before, Liana wasn't sure how to react. Should she play it cool? Act the dumb blonde? Defend herself with a good offense? The last idea appealed most, so she summoned a haughty manner and spoke to the rude giant.

"Are you aware that this is private property, and that you are trespassing?" she inquired coolly.

"I know it's private property," came his sexy, deep-throated reply while his perusing eyes mocked her. "I also know which one of us is trespassing."

His voice sent shivers down Liana's spine, and his meaning was clear. Damn! He had to be the new owner, she surmised grimly. She felt like a thief caught stealing.

She tried not to show her dismay, yet she seethed at the injustice of being caught in so humiliating a situation. Worse, he looked ready to enjoy himself at her expense.

Why wasn't he in New York? Her parents said their new neighbor had visited and then disappeared again. Who'd have thought a busy tycoon would be prowling around a field at this time of the morning? And why didn't he look anything like she had him pictured?

He'd been featured in an article by the local newspaper, but their photo made him look dark and fiftyish while in reality he was blond and thirtyish. She made a mental note never to let them photograph her.

"You're going to wrinkle like a prune," came a low taunt that snapped Liana's attention back to him and made her even more disgruntled.

"I can't get out of the water with you here," she countered. "Why don't you do whatever you came to do and then leave?" The rudeness was uncharacteristic, but she was feeling pretty defensive.

"What if I came for a swim?" he asked softly, his eyes sliding to her awkward position in the water.

Liana tried to cover her breasts while bouncing on tiptoe to keep her mouth above water. The water was crystal-clear. There was no way to adequately shield herself. It was infuriating, and his suggestive tone didn't help matters.

"If you'll allow me some privacy, I promise I'll get out of your way as soon as possible," she managed. "Then you can have the whole pond to yourself!"

"What if I want to share?" he replied smoothly, his eyes gleaming with devilish delight.

"Tough luck," Liana dared.

She probably shouldn't antagonize him, but she was too agitated to think of being tactful. This arrogant giant wanted to provoke her instead of being polite and leaving her in peace.

The newspaper article had hinted that Nate Harden was keen on his own privacy, but he wasn't going to give her any. Her dignity was suffering quite a blow, and she was furious for getting caught in such an embarrassing situation.

"Where did you leave your clothes?" the giant

finally asked, his eyes never straying from Liana's nude form.

"They're right behind you in the grass," she said, not believing he hadn't seen them. He was standing directly in front of the same flat boulder she'd sat on earlier.

A large hand reached across the rock and lifted her bra. "If you mean this flimsy yellow thing," he teased outrageously, "then you'll be nearly as naked after you're dressed as you are now."

The heat in Liana's face grew hotter, and so did her temper. The audacity of the man made her grind her teeth and count to ten. No one had ever humiliated her so thoroughly in such a short span of time. He didn't even try to hide his delight at her predicament.

"My underwear is no concern of yours, Mr. Harden. Just leave, and I'll worry about my clothes."

The giant reluctantly ignored her while searching the area for additional clothing. Liana's eyes searched, too, but there was no sign of her denim shorts and tank top.

She moved closer to the bank as an unwelcome thought took shape in her mind. Smokey was notorious for carrying off her belongings, and she hadn't put everything out of his reach. If he'd made off with her clothes, she'd ring his shaggy neck. Why hadn't she considered the possibility?

"You didn't happen to see a brown and gray Pekingese, did you?" she asked hesitantly. Her question was followed by an instant of total silence and then the explosive sound of masculine laughter.

The deep-throated laugh should have grated on her nerves, yet it shivered over her body like a caress.

Liana didn't care for her primitive response to his rumbling tone.

"You think the situation's so amusing?" she snapped in an attempt to shame him.

The effort failed, and Liana was forced to rein in her temper until his amusement subsided. Then he added fuel to the flames of her anger with his next statement.

"I think your pet is proving to be this man's best friend," he declared with husky enjoyment. Then he was laughing at his own humor.

Liana's eyes narrowed. She moved still closer to the bank so that she could berate him without the risk of swallowing water. The last thing she wanted right now was mouth-to-mouth resuscitation.

"I'm pleased to have supplied you with so much amusement, but if you don't mind, I'd like to get out of the water. You are in my way. Most self-respecting gentlemen would turn their backs or find a way to help me."

Another roar of laughter followed her fruitless attempt to shame him. Liana was shocked at the amount of control she needed to suppress her anger. She was actually trembling. She had an urge to climb nude and dripping from the water and smack his handsome, mocking face.

If the gossips were to be believed, he was no stranger to women. Nudity probably wasn't a novelty for him. It was for her. The thought compounded her humiliation.

She glared at her tormentor, her eyes scouring his features as she assessed him thoroughly. Few men were a real threat once they'd been studied, understood, and categorized. She wanted to immunize herself against this man.

He was startlingly attractive. To her artist's eyes, his body looked sculpted to perfection. His face was tanned and smooth-shaven; his jaws firm and his mouth wide. With his lips parted in a wide grin, he revealed beautiful, straight teeth. The total effect left Liana strangely shaken.

The gleam in his eyes sparked a shiver of awareness that thrilled her, yet fueled her resentment.

"If the thought of gentlemanly behavior causes so much mirth," she tossed at him, "I'll settle for common courtesy."

"Forgive me my shortcomings, nymph," he apologized, with a tremor of amusement lacing his tone. "I'll turn around so that you can put on your . . . er . . . yellow thing. Then I'll play the gentleman and lend you the shirt off my back."

His eyes sparkled, but he turned his back and began to tug the blue chambray shirt from the waistband of faded, snug-fitting jeans.

Liana hesitated. She trusted him, strangely enough, yet she was oddly affected by the intimacy of his actions. He casually stripped off his shirt and exposed a gorgeous breadth of back and shoulder muscles.

She wasn't usually awed by bare torsos, but something deep within her responded to the pure male beauty of this one. The savagely sensual reaction alarmed her and warned her to proceed with caution.

"Are you coming out, nymph?" he cajoled softly. "Or will I turn around and find you've vanished into air?"

"Don't turn around!" Liana exclaimed as she

pulled herself from the water and wriggled into the clinging fabric of her bra. It was flimsy, but preferable to being naked.

After a brief hesitation, she reached out and accepted the shirt offered over his shoulder. It was too big, too long, and disturbingly warm, but it felt good and smelled marvelous.

She struggled with the buttons and had barely fastened the last one when the giant turned. He leisurely surveyed her from the tips of her painted toenails to the hostile brilliance of her eyes.

Liana endured the inspection with as much dignity as possible. She tried to ignore him while wringing some of the excess water from her hair, but it was obvious to both of them that she wanted to get off his property.

"Thank you for the loan of your shirt, Mr. Harden," she said. "I'll clean it and see that it's returned as soon as possible."

"How is it that you know my name, nymph?" he asked as an obvious delaying tactic.

"This is a small, tightly knit community. If you stay around very long, you'll find that everyone knows everyone else, and usually most of their business."

The giant didn't reply, but his features tightened. He apparently didn't like the idea of his personal **busine**ss becoming public knowledge. Too bad.

"If everybody knows everybody else, then why haven't we met?" he taunted.

"I couldn't say," Liana lied.

"Or won't say," he argued, crossing his arms over his chest and causing a natural rippling of muscles. His eyes were more intent now. "You would have to be the Banners' baby girl home from New York for the summer.''

"Would I?''

"I've been gone a few weeks,'' he said, "but if we were both residents of this community, we'd have met.''

Liana flinched at the thought that he might already be well acquainted with her parents. She didn't need any additional aggravation in her life right now.

"You're probably right,'' she told him dismissively. Then she turned toward her dad's property. "I have to go.''

She'd barely taken a step before a strong, tanned hand settled lightly but firmly on her arm, sending a jolt of awareness over her body. She turned, noting that the sprinkling of blond hair on his arm matched the curling mass of hair on his chest and the thick, wavy hair of his head.

"How are you going to explain your state of undress?''

The thought hadn't occurred to her, and she grimaced. This would definitely precipitate another round of scolding and coddling. Lately her parents were smothering her with tender loving care.

"I'm sure no one will be interested,'' she fabricated.

"Liar,'' he mocked softly. "I've gotten to know your parents, and I don't think they'd approve of your skinny-dipping in such an isolated spot.''

"I was not skinny-dipping!'' Liana protested hotly, her face flaming with embarrassment.

The arrogant arching of his brows declared that she might as well have been naked.

"I'm a little old for parental guidance,'' she argued. "I'll just climb back in my window, and they won't know I've been anywhere but the shower."

Stating the newly formed plan aloud made it seem feasible until Nate burst her little bubble of optimism.

"And what if I feel it my neighborly duty to inform them of your dangerous habits?"

"You wouldn't," she challenged.

"I might," he threatened.

"Why?" came Liana's frustrated query. She didn't need added tension between her and her parents.

"I might consider it my moral obligation," he countered suavely.

"Liar," she accused, returning his earlier insult.

The strong column of Nate's throat thrust forward as he threw back his head and roared with laughter. Normally Liana enjoyed an exhilarating exchange of banter and the sound of husky laughter, but nothing about her encounter with Nate Harden felt normal. She was impatient to be gone.

"All right," he confessed when his laughter subsided. "I'm not a strictly moral person, but I'm pretty sure your parents are morally upright."

"So?"

"So what's it worth to keep me quiet?"

Liana glared at him and wondered how serious he was. "I have a feeling I'm about to be either blackmailed or compromised."

She knew her declaration appealed to his warped sense of humor, but she gave him credit for controlling his amusement this time.

TWO

"I've already admitted that I'm immoral," he reminded.

"What could you possibly want from a total stranger, Mr. Harden?"

Nate's eyes narrowed as he brazenly scrutinized the appealing picture of femininity she presented.

Liana felt her blood pressure skyrocketing, and she clamped her teeth shut in frustration. She refused to comment on his blatantly sexual appraisal.

"I'll keep quiet on three conditions," he told her.

"Conditions! What kind of conditions do you think I'd be willing to accept?" She should tell him to go to hell, but feminine curiosity kept her rooted to the spot.

"First," he outlined, undaunted by her glowering eyes, "my friends call me Nate, and I want us to be friends."

Liana seriously doubted it, but if calling him by his first name would keep him quiet, then she could manage to be civil. Hardly anyone in this area stood on formalities.

"Nate it is," she agreed, turning away again and attempting to put some distance between them.

"Don't be in such a hurry, nymph." His soft tone halted her escape. "I said three conditions."

Liana kept her back to him. "What are the other two conditions?" she heard herself asking.

"One, the name is Nate. Two, I want your promise not to swim here alone. And three, I want a promise that you'll have dinner with me sometime very soon."

Liana turned and stared at him in amazement, her expression revealing her distaste for the final condition.

"Now, see here Mr. . . . Nate," she corrected swiftly. "I have no objection to calling you by your first name, and I'd die before I'd hazard a repeat performance of this morning's fiasco, but I won't be blackmailed into accepting a date from someone I don't even—"

Liana's tirade was interrupted by a series of sharp barks alerting them to Smokey's whereabouts. She and Nate simultaneously turned to see the little dog standing close to the boundary fence. He was proudly displaying his catch for the morning: a pair of shorts and a yellow top.

"Smokey, you rotten little thief!" Liana shouted in irritation. "You leave my clothes right there!"

The pooch barked an excited refusal, then snatched her clothes and dashed under the fence. Liana had a mental image of him presenting them to her mother and dad.

"Smokey, stop!" she screamed as she ran after him.

An amused Nate joined the procession.

Liana's only hope was that Smokey would enjoy the chase so much that he'd drop his burden. What she hadn't considered was her own clumsiness while hindered by Nate's shirt flapping about her knees, her tender feet, and her limited capabilities in the heat.

Nate's proximity and amusement added another disadvantage. He was a very disturbing nuisance.

A short distance from the fence, Liana's right foot came down on a large, prickly thistle. She screeched in pain, grabbed her injured foot with both hands, and hopped around wildly, causing her to collide head-on with Nate.

The force of the collision sent them crashing to the ground with a heavy thud. Nate's arms closed protectively around Liana and broke her fall, but they were both temporarily stunned and winded.

The physical exertion, the fierce heat, and the added weight of Nate's body left Liana gasping for air. Her hands came up to push him away, but she was surprised by the jolt of pleasure she experienced from touching the crisp curls on his solid chest. She moaned at the increasing absurdity of her predicament and closed her eyes to hide temporarily.

Nate shifted his weight to his forearms and planted them on either side of her head. He lifted his chest enough to allow her breathing space, but he kept most of his body pressed to hers. He wasn't in any hurry to break the contact between them.

Slowly Liana's long lashes swept up and her wary, somewhat bemused eyes encountered the jeweled brilliance of the turquoise-green eyes so very near her own.

Bedroom eyes, she mused, hypnotized by the truly gorgeous eyes regarding her so steadily. She'd heard people describe eyes in such a fashion, and now she understood the description. Nate's gaze had become warm and caressive while the sun trapped her own image in their sparkling depths. The sensual shock was like nothing she'd ever experienced.

Her labored breathing stilled somewhat, but an entirely different type of pounding began to throb throughout her body. It was like the steadily increasing tempo of pagan drums that might be heard on an island paradise. The hypnotic rhythm pulsed throughout her body.

Time ceased to matter as Liana's senses absorbed the sounds of crackling dew on the grass, the throbbing heat of the sun, and the intensity of Nate's gaze as he scrutinized her flushed features.

Now Nate understood why Dave Banner's eyes always sparkled when he spoke of his youngest daughter. She was proud, spirited, and incredibly beautiful. Her complexion was flawless, her eyes wide, bright blue and framed with thick, sooty lashes. Her nose was small and straight. The tantalizing fullness of her mouth made him ache to know if it felt as soft as it looked.

He'd seen dozens of pictures of Liana, and he'd listened to the pride in her parents' voices when they spoke of her. He'd been intrigued, but nothing had prepared him for the very real, very feminine Liana Banner.

She thought his hair was the color of old gold. It was thick, just a bit long, with springy waves that made her want to run her fingers through it. His jawbones were high and strong, hinting at a character of equal strength.

His strong, hard body created an ache in her that was totally foreign. She wanted to touch him, explore him, and that alarmed her.

Her lashes swept down to conceal the shocking effect his nearness was having on her. Nate's warm breath mingled with hers for an instant before his mouth brushed her lips in a seductively sweet plea for cooperation. He wanted a kiss.

He was bold, brash, and impossibly arrogant for asking, yet he asked so nicely. Liana slowly opened her eyes once more.

She suspected she was finally losing her sanity. She was a fool for not immediately scrambling to her feet. Years of lectures, warnings, and self-defense instructions slipped her mind. She was utterly fascinated by a total stranger.

His eyes searched hers, and he looked just as enthralled as she was. His head dipped to block out the sun, and he tickled her lips with his own. Liana's resistance was nonexistent. Her lips softened and parted on a sigh.

His lips continued to coax and woo as if time had lost all meaning. His teeth nibbled gently on the curve of her lower lip, and the very tip of his tongue tickled its way over the pearly smoothness of her teeth. Liana's pulse rate quickened, and she opened her lips wider.

Nate was happy to take advantage of her tiny action of surrender. His mouth pressed firmly against hers, and they shared a long, searching kiss that was so sweetly sensitive, it left them both hungry for more.

After the briefest hesitation, Liana slid her arms along his shoulders to the strong column of his neck. She locked them lightly, pulling him a bit closer, and returned his kiss without shyness or pretension. Her curiosity was aroused by his gentleness, and begged for satisfaction.

Nate didn't need much encouragement to deepen the kiss, and his tongue parted her lips with carefully restrained patience.

He wanted a more thorough exploration of her responsive mouth. He'd been aching for closer contact since he'd first caught sight of her in the water.

He'd been captivated by her grace, her natural beauty, and her exquisite body. Darkened by water, her hair looked like raw silver. Her skin was a delicate golden shade except for the paleness of areas that were normally denied exposure to the sun.

He'd known that she would resent his presence, but he hadn't found the strength or chivalry to walk away. Her playfulness, and later her sensual sunning, had enthralled him as nothing else in his life had ever done.

When his mouth briefly left Liana's, his lips continued to explore her face, brushing tender kisses over her fluttering eyelids and the delicate curve of her cheeks.

Then he recaptured her mouth in another deep kiss, his tongue delving, dueling, and delighting hers. Her hold on him tightened ever so slightly, but it was enough to make fire lick through his veins.

Deep within Liana, her conservative subconscious was aghast. Nate Harden was no innocent schoolboy, and she was a fool for not putting a stop to this seduction of senses.

Instead, she absorbed the feel of him and ignored the mental warnings. Her arms tightened, and her mouth responded to the mastery of his.

Right or wrong, she gloried in the rapture of the moment, and she didn't want to put a stop to their embrace.

His big, slightly rough hands began a slow investigation of her back. First he gently stroked her through the cotton of his shirt, but then his caressing fingers slipped beneath the fabric to seek out bare flesh.

Liana gasped in surprise as bare flesh met bare flesh, but Nate's tongue challenged hers at the same instant and made her momentarily forget what his hands were doing.

She recognized the sensual expertise and knew she was being caressed by experienced hands, yet was thrilled rather than apprehensive as his warm fingers kneaded her spine.

Nate moaned low in his throat as he massaged the smooth, satin flesh of her back. All the blood in his body rushed to his groin. Their lower bodies were locked so tightly that he couldn't conceal his growing arousal, but he remained perfectly still instead of trying to ease the ache.

He didn't want to frighten her. He sensed that she was just as captivated as he was, so he didn't want to do anything to cause her to reject his tentative explorations.

His mouth continued to tenderly devour Liana's as his hands grew impatient for the feel of his breasts. He'd been mesmerized earlier at the sight of her pagan beauty, and now he wanted to explore the feminine softness. The need was shocking in its intensity.

Liana remained inexplicably fearless in a potentially dangerous situation. She felt weak and vulnerable in this stranger's arms, yet more alive than she'd felt for months. Her breathing faltered a little as she felt the undeniable strength of Nate's arousal, but she still didn't call a halt to what was happening between them. It felt so right

Despite her natural instinct for caution, Liana wasn't afraid of Nate. She should have been stunned by her violent reactions, but she felt curiously safe and secure in his arms. For a short time she chose to enjoy the taste, smell, and feel of this incredibly attractive stranger.

She involuntarily squirmed beneath Nate's weight, and he groaned into her mouth. His hands tightened at her waist, then slowly moved over her rib cage to her damp bra. Her flesh was cool, but unbelievably soft. When his fingers brushed her breasts, her nipples tightened immediately, and Nate's arousal burgeoned in reaction.

A shudder of pleasure ripped through his body, and primitive yearning clutched at his heart. He swallowed her cry of surprise and plunged his tongue deeper into her mouth. He felt a savage satisfaction when she trembled. The claim he was staking was elemental, and as necessary as his next breath. Nate had never considered himself a possessive man, but no woman had ever touched him as deeply as this one was doing now.

Liana was shocked by the wild thrill she experienced when he touched her, so she swiftly dragged his hands from her body. How could this stranger make her feel a quicksilver pleasure that no other man had ever supplied? What was happening to her?

What was she allowing to happen? She could feel his bold reaction to their embrace, and she knew she had to defuse the highly volatile situation.

Liana flattened her hands on his chest and gently shoved. Her own hands trembled slightly as they met the hard warmth of his body. Her eyes were fathomless pools of blue.

They gazed at each other for a long, intense moment. Nate's body tightened painfully as he recognized the turbulence in her sapphire blue eyes. She studied him with a fascination that he shared. The wonder in her eyes was rare, and he felt himself falling hard, very hard, into an emotional trap that he'd thought himself destined to escape.

"You're very beautiful," he declared hoarsely. She was sunshine and warmth and sensuality.

"So are you," Liana returned honestly. She thought he was beautiful, and not just because of his physical looks. He'd halted his intimate caresses at the first sign of her objection, and his touch was so very gentle. He hadn't tried to take advantage of her unexpected vulnerability, and he wasn't enraged by her withdrawal.

"Why?" she asked him huskily, her eyes beseeching him to explain the explosive attraction between them.

A sexy, roguish smile curved Nate's mouth. He understood her confusion and concern. "Some people call it animal magnetism, some attribute it to body chemistry," he said, his eyes holding her unblinking gaze while his fingers combed through her hair.

"Others call it kismet, or fate." This last was a whisper as his lips sought Liana's for a kiss that set their hearts pounding.

Nate put both arms around her again, cradling her against his chest. He was content to feel her warmth through the thin fabric of his shirt. He wanted more, so much more, but he had no right to ask for it.

Liana sank her fingers into the thickness of his hair and clutched his head until their mouths parted for breath.

"I want to get to know you," he murmured as he caressed her face with warm lips. "I'd like to make love to you right here, right now, but I can wait. Promise me you won't deny this need."

His certainty that they'd become lovers shocked Liana as nothing else had. A clear, condemning vision of Rod flashed into her muddled thoughts, and she slowly pulled her arms from Nate's neck. She continued to hold his gaze, but mentally commanded her body to withdraw.

Nate shifted his weight and rolled to one side, but he didn't relinquish his hold on her. "Why the sudden tension?" he asked gruffly. He didn't like her withdrawal or the wariness that entered her eyes.

"We're total strangers!" Liana felt compelled to remind.

"We might be strangers in relation to the length of our acquaintance, but we're basically like all other creatures seeking mates. Time has no meaning. The attraction is what's important."

"You really believe that?" His attitude certainly defied the conventionalism she was accustomed to.

"Do you deny that your body is aching for mine as much as mine aches for you?"

Liana didn't deny it. She was racking her brain for an explanation. It was probably due to a serious lack of male attention. She'd been ill and hadn't been held or kissed for months. She'd never been kissed as Nate kissed her, but she didn't want to dwell on that right now.

"Wanting doesn't make it acceptable."

"Then what does?" he asked very seriously.

Liana searched for the right answer. "Caring, mutual respect, emotional commitment," she enumerated.

"And what good are all those without desire?" he wanted to know.

"Desire goes hand in hand with the others," she insisted, wanting to clarify her belief for both of them.

Nate shook his head. He didn't share her views. "You're really a naive little goose if you believe that."

Liana bristled at his tone and blushed at the accuracy of his comment. She wasn't naive, but she was woefully inexperienced, and he probably suspected as much.

She also resented his cynicism after such tender loving. His gentle approach apparently stemmed from vast experience, not innate sensitivity.

"I think I prefer real emotion to cynical indifference," she said as she disentangled herself from his embrace and rose to her feet.

"You think I'm indifferent to you?" taunted Nate as he rose from the ground.

"I think you're an experienced seducer, but I doubt that you're looking for a meaningful relationship."

She was right, but Nate resented her quick assessment of his character. He'd never wanted commitment, yet he'd never met a woman who made as savage an impact as Liana.

"And what would it take to win your heart, Miss Liana Marie Banner?"

Liana blushed in confusion and agitation. He knew more about her than she'd thought. There was no telling how much her parents had divulged about her personal life.

"My heart is promised to another man, Mr. Nate Harden," she told him firmly. "It's not up for grabs."

Her declaration sent a wave of dark emotion washing over Nate. Jealousy—swift, hot, and fierce—defied his lifelong policy of emotional detachment.

"Who is he?"

The question was so harsh that Liana stepped farther from him. Her pulse quickened at the thought that he might really care.

"His name is Rod Govern."

Nate hated the way her voice softened on the other man's name, but he forced himself to relax. The Banners had told him about Liana's lifelong sweetheart. He'd seen photos of them together, but the looks they gave each other spoke of affection, not passion. "Where is he?"

"He's been working in South America. His project's done, so I expect him to be home any day." Liana needed to erect barriers.

"Then what?"

She frowned at the question and self-consciously flipped her tousled hair over her shoulders. She hadn't the slightest idea what would happen when Rod returned, but she didn't want to discuss her doubts. It really wasn't any concern of his.

"I have to get back to the house," she said, ignoring his challenging expression. She turned without another word.

"Liana." Nate made her name sound like a silken promise. "Don't forget those three conditions I mentioned."

She tensed and halted, refusing to comment.

"Be especially careful to honor condition number two. If I ever find you swimming here alone, I'll do worse than tell your parents."

He didn't elaborate, and she didn't demand details.

"If you'd picked tomorrow morning for your solitary swim, you'd have had a brutal interruption. There's a construction crew scheduled to come at daybreak."

His words alarmed Liana enough to make her turn and stare at him. The mention of construction at this heavenly oasis sent a chill over her. Images of concrete and steel flashed into her mind, and she glared at Nate.

"What are you going to do to the pond?"

"What business is it of yours?"

Liana clenched her teeth. It was none of her business. "There are zoning laws in this area. You have to have special permission to alter land that's zoned for farming."

Nate's eyes took on a mocking glint. "I have permission for my project," he told her, then decided that he didn't want her to think of him as a despoiler of beauty.

"The crew will be laying tile to pipe some of the springwater toward the homestead," he explained.

Liana felt relieved, but foolish. Mr. Drenasis had planned to do the tile work, but never got around to it. She could stop acting like an environmental activist.

"You're a rotten tease," she accused.

Nate didn't deny it. He was troubled by the conflicting need either to alienate this lovely woman or completely possess her. She was all wrong for him. She was sunshine; a small-town princess, cheerleader, homecoming queen, all-American sweetheart.

His life was filled with shadows. If any of his new neighbors delved too deeply into his background, they were likely to open a Pandora's box of pain, bitterness, and resentment. His past could destroy any chance he had for acceptance in the near future. He needed to alienate his lovely new acquaintance before the fascination had a chance to blossom.

"You're a tease, too," he countered roughly. The sight of her in his favorite shirt was wildly arousing. "Do you have any idea how sexy you look at this minute?"

Liana's eyes widened, and she crossed her arms protectively over her breasts. She felt disheveled and bereft of appeal, but she didn't dispute his claim.

"I have to go. I'll return your shirt," she replied, turning from him. She climbed the fence and headed toward home without a backward glance, but felt the heat of Nate's eyes following her out of sight.

Halfway through the woods, she found and donned her own clothes. Smokey had obviously lost interest in the game when she'd failed to follow him, and she was thankful for small favors. She had enough problems at present without adding her parents' disapproval.

She was unusually quiet the rest of the day. The exertion of the morning left her weary, and thoughts of Nate Harden were tumultuous. She had a feeling that her life was about to be totally disrupted. Earlier in the day she'd have welcomed the thought. Now she wasn't so sure she wanted dramatic changes in her life-style.

THREE

It was early the next morning when Liana kicked off the sheet cloaking her nudity. Sleeping naked was the latest maneuver in her private war against the oppressive heat. A very pleasant one, too, she thought with a grin. Not quite so pleasant as swimming in the nude, but that particular battle had proved too much for her with the interference of a highly experienced opponent.

Her toes curled and warmth stole over her body at the thought of her encounter with Nate Harden. Just the memory of his touch set her pulse pounding erratically and threatened her composure.

As hard as she'd tried yesterday and last night, she couldn't erase the image of those gorgeous bedroom eyes just before the lids lowered and his mouth captured hers in the sweetest, sexiest kisses she'd ever known.

What had possessed her to behave in such a wanton fashion? Was she really that desperate for masculine attention? Or was Nate an absolute master of seduction?

To be honest, it hadn't been necessary for him to do much seducing. She'd been putty in his hands, she thought in disgust. She was usually slow to respond to any man's advances, and she never allowed herself to become deeply involved, so what was special about Nate?

Questions, questions, questions, and no answers. Another restless night hadn't improved her disposition.

"Liana, breakfast is ready!" called her mother.

She wasn't very hungry. The heat and humidity had zapped her appetite, yet she knew her parents would fret if she didn't make an appearance at the table.

Climbing from bed, she slipped on panties and a white terry robe that barely covered her hips. It was worn and thin, but it would suffice for breakfast. Nobody should expect perfection first thing in the morning. After running a brush haphazardly through her hair, she decided she looked acceptable, if not quite respectable.

She descended the stairs and made her way through the long hall to the back of the house where the kitchen ran full length of the building.

Then she got her first shock of the day. Sitting beside her father at the table was their newest neighbor. It was a supreme effort to retain her dignity.

The men paused in the conversation, and Nate started to rise, but Liana waved away his polite gesture and quickly seated herself. She forced herself not to blush or pull her robe more tightly about her unbound breasts.

"Good morning, sweetheart." Dave Banner's tone

held its usual mixture of pride and warmth. "We should have warned you that we had company. I've wanted to introduce you to Nate, but he told me you'd met. Now that he's back in Springdale, you'll get used to seeing him at our table."

Liana sincerely doubted it. There was nothing remotely comfortable about Nate Harden's presence. His eyes seared her, and the tension between them was thick, even if her father didn't notice it.

"I can't think of a better place to be," Nate declared with a genuine smile for Dave and Gloria.

"There isn't a better cook this side of the Mississippi," Dave boasted of his wife.

"Thank you, dear," she replied. Despite early hours and hectic schedules, Gloria Banner always looked neat and attractive. Her blond hair had gone silver, and her figure wasn't as petite as it used to be, but she was still an exceptionally attractive woman.

Gloria handed Liana a plate of bacon, eggs, and toast, then offered her cheek for a kiss. Liana inwardly groaned at the amount of food her mother expected her to eat, but thanked her warmly and pressed a kiss to her cheek.

"Gloria and I raised three beautiful daughters, Nate, and we had two of them married off before any man was allowed to see how mussed and heavy-eyed they look in the morning. Now Liana has upset the apple cart," her dad teased. He was very adept at the art.

"Good morning to you, too, Daddy," she tossed back at him. "The next time you want to exhibit me at the breakfast table, you'd better give me some warning."

Her dad chuckled. Her ability to return his banter

always amused him. Liana munched on a piece of bacon and finally allowed her eyes to meet Nate's steady gaze.

"Besides, I'm sure Nate has seen his share of women across the breakfast table," she dared with a cool smile.

Blue eyes clashed with turquoise-green ones, and the atmosphere became charged. Nate was already a victim of tension. Liana's slumberous beauty made his body tighten with hunger. His eyes managed to convey the message without alerting her parents.

Liana shifted her eyes back to her plate as a tremor of awareness coursed through her. She battled a blush while her mother readily came to Nate's defense.

"You're wrong, Liana," Gloria said in her calm, innocent manner. "Nate is an only child, and his mother's company is probably the only experience he's had with women this early in the morning."

Liana nearly choked on her orange juice. She searched her mother's features, but found no hint of mischief. Rolling her eyes, she noted Nate's amused smile and then her father's devilishly gleaming eyes.

"I'd think after thirty-some years of marriage, you would have explained the facts of life to her," she whispered in a loud aside to her dad. She wondered, yet again, if her mother's naïveté was natural or contrived to entertain her husband. He got such a kick out of her outrageous comments.

Dave just grinned and allowed his eyes to rest on his wife. Liana witnessed the look of adoration he gave Gloria and felt a bit envious. Her parents were fortunate to have a lifetime bond based on love and respect. She wondered if she'd ever find a similar happiness.

"Your mother's right, you know," Nate interjected. The truth was, he'd never lived with a woman and had never chosen to stay with one throughout the night. Seeing Liana this morning made him believe he could thoroughly enjoy the experience. "I'm an only child and unaccustomed to feminine attention."

He sounded so sincere that Liana nearly choked again. His tone was innocent, but his eyes mocked her, daring her not to believe. He probably had women drooling over him. His abundance of sex appeal was indecent.

A shocking thought popped into Liana's mind. "You're not married and never have been?"

"I never seemed to find the time," he supplied, his eyes telling her she was a little late in asking.

Liana gave her breakfast her complete attention. She didn't need any reminders of her wanton behavior. She hadn't forgotten for a moment. Her mind kept drifting to a field of clover and his hard, warm body.

"Did you take care of all your business in New York?" Dave asked, temporarily distracting Nate.

"Most of the legal problems are resolved, and I've moved my belongings, but Mom won't be ready to move for a month or so."

"She'll be joining you soon?" Gloria asked, with such enthusiasm that Liana's curiosity was piqued.

"You know Nate's mother?"

Gloria shot a strange look at Nate, and he gave a slight nod of approval, making Liana doubly curious.

"Nate's mother was my best friend during our teenage years. She's originally from Springdale and wants to move back. I just can't wait to see her again.''

Nate's smile for Gloria was so warm that it made Liana's heart do a little somersault. Her senses were highly attuned to his every emotion.

''You've bought the Drenasis property for your mother?'' she asked.

''For my mother and me,'' he corrected, his smile cool.

''But I thought your work was in New York,'' Liana declared. She'd never imagined that this disturbing hunk of manhood intended to take up residency in Springdale.

''I've just concluded the sale of most of my business interests. Now I'm going into farming full scale.''

A farmer! Liana's eyes shouted her disbelief. She couldn't see how a high-powered business tycoon would be content to devote his life to the backbreaking, unpredictable, and sometimes hazardous chore of farming.

''Are you planning to do some developing in this area?'' She sought a viable explanation.

''No.'' Nate's tone was clipped, his demeanor growing cool. ''I sold my interests in the hotel industry, and I've severed ties with the business community.'' He supposed she found his decision hard to understand, but she didn't know how much he hated city life.

It took Liana a few minutes to digest that distressing bit of information. The man was definitely a threat to her emotional well-being.

''Not everyone is so keen for the city,'' Liana's

father reminded in exasperation. "The country life is growing more appealing all the time."

Liana didn't want to argue country versus city. She loved both, but the city offered the career opportunities she needed. She didn't condemn Nate's choice, but she wondered how she could survive the entire summer with him so close.

"I'm just delighted that you're coming home," Gloria told Nate with heartfelt enthusiasm. Her attitude made Liana wonder why the two mothers hadn't kept in touch if they'd been such good friends.

The phone rang before she could voice the question. Excusing herself, she moved into the hallway and answered the summons. Then she greeted her best friend, Jamie Smith.

Jamie was her lifelong pal. She lived in the village of Springdale, next door to the Govern family. For years she'd supplied inside information about Rod's activities.

"He's home!" Jamie exclaimed in excitement.

"Rod's home? When?" Liana insisted. "How long has he been here? Have you talked to him?"

"I talked to him a little last night when he got in," Jamie told her. "He was exhausted and wanted to get some sleep before he came to see you, but he's on his way now."

"Now! Jamie, you're an angel!" Liana swore. "I have to get dressed and fix my hair. I look like death!"

"You'd better hurry."

"Talk to you later," Liana promised as she hung up and dashed toward the staircase.

"Rod's home! That was Jamie, and Rod's home. He's on his way out here!" she shouted at her parents as she bounded up the stairs. All thoughts of the disturbing man in the kitchen were momentarily wiped from her mind as she anticipated her reunion with Rod.

The guest at the table tensed as he heard the excitement in Liana's voice. He was well aware of Dave and Gloria's speculative gazes, but he couldn't control the grimness that settled over his features. He decided to stick around and meet the competition.

Much later that day, Liana and Rod rocked gently on the front porch swing, with his arm about her shoulders and her head nestled against his chest. Liana sighed with contentment at the lovely day they'd spent.

They'd had so much to talk about and so many things to discuss about their respective careers. It had been a day of laughter, reminiscing, and sharing that displayed how much they'd missed each other.

Liana felt secure in Rod's arms. He offered no threat to her peace of mind. His kisses were warm and soothing, not hot and provocative. His dark-eyed smile was tender and teasing, not bold and challenging.

She'd loved Rod as long as she could remember, and she didn't want anyone threatening those feelings. She was aggravated by the many times her thoughts had flashed to a green-eyed giant, and she resented the fact that Nate Harden's image wasn't easily erased from her mind.

"Your new neighbor is going to disrupt Springdale's staid society," Rod said as he gently stroked Liana's cheek. She stiffened at the mention of Nate.

"I can't believe he's serious about settling here,"

she returned. She hadn't been pleased when Nate had insisted on meeting Rod. She just wanted him to disappear.

"He sounded pretty sure of himself, and seems the type who knows exactly what he wants."

"And gets it," Liana growled.

"He wants you," Rod stated laconically.

Liana tensed. "What makes you say that?"

"The way he watched you this morning," Rod explained. "You barely glanced at him, but his eyes never left you. He made me feel like I was the outsider, and he was the man in possession."

Liana pulled free of his arm and glared at him. "In possession?" She resented the phrasing and the fact that Rod had been aware of the undercurrents between her and Nate.

Rod laughed softly and pulled her back into his arms.

"It's just an expression, sweetheart, but I didn't mean to be offensive. Your new friend struck me as the possessive sort."

"He's not my friend," she countered firmly. "I just met him yesterday."

That surprised Rod. "He seemed prefectly at home here, and more than a little fond of you."

"I guess he's gotten to know my family pretty well," Liana explained. "He's spent a lot of time here, but he was in New York when I came home, and he just returned. I think Mother and Daddy have given him a blow-by-blow account of my life from the time I was a toddler."

Rod chuckled. "They adore you. It's only natural that they sing your praises to newcomers."

Liana grunted her disapproval, and Rod tipped her

head up to plant a kiss on her lips. They were interrupted by a discreet cough at the door.

"Excuse me, I won't intrude long," said Gloria, putting her head out the screen door. "I just wanted to make sure you invited Rod to our party tomorrow evening."

Liana drew away from Rod and stared at her mother in exasperation. "Mother, if we're having a party tomorrow night, then I haven't even been invited."

Gloria seemed mildly surprised. "I've been planning it for some time," she explained. "Did I forget to mention it?"

Liana felt tremors from Rod's silent laughter. "You were probably afraid the anticipation would overstress me," she said.

"Your father and I thought it would be nice to have a barbecue and invite some friends to meet Nate. He's really very shy and hasn't met many of our neighbors."

Nate Harden shy? Liana couldn't believe what she was hearing. "You're having a party for Nate? Why can't someone else introduce him to the community?"

"Because we're his nearest neighbors, and we know him better than anyone else. I want to make him feel at home."

"I think I may have a serious relapse," grumbled Liana.

"Shame on you," her mother scolded, then turned her attention to Rod. "Don't you forget, Rodney. We'll be eating about eight, so come early and bring Jamie with you."

"Will do," Rod agreed, amusement still threading

his tone. He squeezed Liana gently, then teased her when her mother left.

"I'd almost forgotten how traditional life is in Springdale. If a respected adult tells you to do something, you do it, no argument."

"I just wonder how much longer it's going to take before I'm considered a respected adult," Liana commented.

"Another decade or two," Rod supplied, and then hugged her. "You said you were bored, and you love parties, so you ought to enjoy a barbecue."

"Not if it means several hours in Nate Harden's company."

"He bothers you that much?" Rod probed quietly.

Liana didn't like the direction of his thoughts. "I can't help it if I took an immediate dislike to my mother's fair-haired boy."

"You must have."

Liana let the subject drop and squirmed closer to him. She wanted to forget Nate and concentrate on the comfort of Rod's arms. She tried to relax, but she couldn't seem to sit still.

"Ease up, honey," Rod murmured as he brushed a kiss across her forehead. "I'm trying to seduce you with my abundance of charm, and you're too restless to notice."

Liana smiled into his eyes, but didn't relax. "I'm sorry. I do love your charming ways, but I can't get comfortable tonight."

"What's wrong?"

"I itch!" She tried to ease her discomfort by rubbing against him. She was serious, but he roared with laughter. Somehow their seduction scenes always erupted into laughter.

* * *

The itching was very real and very, very irritating. Liana was miserable for the rest of the night. When she awoke the next morning, she stood before her mirror and tried to identify the red, burning rash covering her entire midsection.

"Poison ivy," her mother diagnosed after examining the rash.

"Poison ivy? I haven't had it in years!"

"I know, dear, but some people never build up a resistance. You must have brushed against some vines while you were walking through the woods. Your father says it's thick this year."

Liana heaved a sigh. She was red, front and back, from breast to hip, and she'd made herself sore by scratching all night. She was never going to be able to stand clothing.

"What can I do?"

"First you need to scrub your hands and stop touching it so you don't spread the poison. I have some lotion that will ease the itching and help dry the rash. It's best to cover the infected area with a light bandage, but I don't think that's possible."

Liana grimaced at the image of herself bound like a mummy. "Maybe I can get by with a long cotton T-shirt."

"That sounds best. Try not to get hot or sweaty," her mother advised. "Stay out of the sun today or you'll irritate your skin even more."

"Okay," Liana agreed, then she had a glimmer of inspiration. "There's no way I can help with the party tonight. Maybe I'll stay in my room and read. That way I won't have to worry about clothes or infecting our guests."

Gloria gave her a reproving glance and headed for her closet. "There's absolutely no reason for you to miss the party. I'm sure you have something that's both suitable and comfortable."

"I can't even wear a bra, Mother," Liana protested. "If I go braless, I'll shock our guests and simply ruin my reputation!"

"Nonsense." Her mother wasn't fooled by that ploy. "You're a little large to go without a bra, but you have high, firm breasts, so you can get away with a braless style."

Together they searched Liana's wardrobe until they found a dress that suited their need. It was powder blue, and the style was simple. The shoulder straps were narrow and tied with bows to form the armholes. The rest of the dress was a full and flowing shift that covered her from breast to below the knees. Normally Liana wore it belted at the waist, but she could let it swirl loosely around her.

"If I wear it without a belt, everyone will swear I'm pregnant and I've come home to have my illegitimate baby."

Gloria clucked her tongue, but didn't argue. Some people were always hungry for a juicy piece of gossip. Liana had chosen to live in New York, so she would be watched more closely by the locals.

"You've been home a month, and people will believe what they want. Time has a way of discouraging that sort of gossip."

"I suppose," Liana murmured. She'd sworn years ago to discount what the gossips whispered, but living at home had renewed her sensitivity to the rumor mill.

She spent most of the day helping her mother and

then managed a long nap in the afternoon. Feeling refreshed, she began to look forward to the party and even hummed cheerfully while she showered and had anti-itch lotion smoothed over her infected flesh.

Her hair was long and baby-fine, so she usually had to bind it in some fashion. While it was still damp from washing, she wove a braid down her back and then twisted the braid into a chignon at her nape.

The style suited her. It was simple but elegant, and it gave her self-confidence a much-needed boost.

At home she seemed to lack the sophisticated poise that came so easily in New York. After weeks of debilitating illness and a month of her parents' fussing, she felt more insecure than she ever had during her teenage years.

When applying her makeup, she spent an unusual amount of time highlighting her eyes. The action reminded her of Nate Harden's eyes, and the hand wielding her mascara wand trembled slightly. She refused to believe that her increasing excitement had anything to do with seeing him.

She couldn't help comparing Rod and Nate. She knew she shouldn't, but they battled for equal time in her thoughts. Rod was everything she wanted in a man. He was sweet, intelligent, sensitive, and shared her lively sense of humor. They'd always known they were well suited for each other.

Liana had hoped that their reunion might spark more passion between them, but it hadn't happened. Passion wasn't everything.

Nate Harden had inflamed her in a sensual, passionate fashion, yet he was a stranger. She had to be careful not to let her body's reaction to his magnetism overrule her common sense.

Maybe she could convince Jamie to show Nate a little extra attention. Her best friend had a fabulous personality. She was lovely and lively. Nate was sure to like Jamie; everybody liked her. Great.

Well, maybe not so great, Liana thought as she headed downstairs to help her parents. For some reason she didn't like the idea of Nate and Jamie becoming involved. Maybe it was just her suspicion that Nate wasn't the type to risk romantic attachments. She didn't want to see Jamie get hurt.

FOUR

"What can I do?" Liana asked, entering the kitchen.

Gloria was wearing a pink halter dress that enhanced her smooth, lightly tanned skin and fair coloring. Dave, a head taller and very lean, was dressed in his favorite jeans and a pullover knit shirt. He was darkly tanned, and his skin was an attractive contrast to his pale blond hair.

"You can help me," he said while carrying a load of barbecue utensils out the back door.

"I want her to stay inside," Gloria declared without explaining. "She can help with hors d'oeuvres."

"What's on the menu?" Liana asked.

"Your dad's grilling steaks, pork chops, and hamburgers. He's roasting potatoes and corn in the barbecue pit. The drinks are on ice, so all we need to worry about is a vegetable tray and some appetizers."

"What about dessert?"

"The ladies from my card club volunteered to bake pies. Jamie's bringing a Texas sheet cake, and I have dozens of cookies that can come out of the freezer if we need them."

"Sounds like everything's well in hand," Liana commented as she began to roll candied dill pickles in slices of baked ham that were garnished with cream cheese. "You've always had a talent for organization."

"I've needed it," Gloria said. "Being a farm wife takes a multitude of skills, and there's always more work than time."

"Excelling at anything takes time and determination."

"You've accomplished wonders in your career," Gloria praised. "But I'd prefer you were successful and healthy."

"So would I." Liana knew she'd needed this rest, but she still had to battle the frustration of curtailing her career for an entire summer. It was only June. Her high spirits drooped a little until she heard a familiar voice at the front door.

"Anybody home?"

"We're in the kitchen, Jamie!"

"Hi there," Jamie said as she entered the room and placed a cake on the dessert table. "You two sure look smashing," she added as she gave each of them a brief hug.

"If I'd known you were going to look so feminine and sophisticated, I'd have worn a dress," she told Liana in her lilting tone. "I feel dowdy in my jeans and shirt."

"Your designer jeans and chic silk blouse," Liana

admired. Jamie's petite figure looked great in jeans. The yellow of her blouse enhanced the rich color of her auburn curls and dark eyes. "You look pretty dazzling yourself."

"A dazzling country girl while you're a sophisticated knockout in that dress."

"If I had my druthers, I'd druther be in jeans," Liana told her.

"Poor Liana was forced to wear a dress," Gloria injected. "She couldn't stand the agony of tight clothes."

Jamie was immediately concerned. "Agony? Have you hurt yourself?"

"I've got poison ivy all . . . over . . . my . . . body!" Liana drawled dramatically. "My midsection is blistered, and I didn't have much choice of party clothes."

Jamie laughed at her clowning. Then she apologized. "I'm sorry. I know it's no fun to have poison ivy, but you suffer with such dignity."

"Thanks," Liana quipped. "Your sense of humor is warped."

Jamie contained her amusement while scrutinizing Liana thoroughly. "I don't see any signs of a rash."

"It starts below the neckline and ends at my waist."

"How in the world did you manage that?"

"Who knows? I have the luck of the condemned lately."

"Maybe things will improve now that Rod's home."

"Speaking of Rod," chimed Gloria, "wasn't he supposed to come with you?"

Liana was looking directly at Jamie and was surprised when she blushed. Were she and Rod at odds with each other? The three of them had always been best of friends.

"I wanted to drive my own car. I think he's coming with his parents."

Before Liana could comment about the sudden tension in her friend, they heard several voices blending with Dave's on the patio. Their guests were arriving.

"We'd better go out," Gloria declared as she put the final touches on a tray of hors d'oeuvres.

Liana and Jamie followed her out the sliding doors to the patio area, where a considerable number of people swarmed, all talking and laughing.

Liana groaned and stayed close to the door. Now that she was actually faced with so many people, she wasn't sure she was up to this affair. "It's going to be a long night."

"Your mother probably only invited a couple hundred people who will want an hour-by-hour, day-to-day account of your life in New York," Jamie teased.

Liana groaned again. "The first thing they'll ask is when the baby's due and why I'm not wearing a bra," she surmised, feeling slightly self-conscious.

Jamie's response was whispered for her ears only. "I still think you should share your abundance with me. I'm braless, and no one will notice. When you go braless, it's bound to cause a stir. We could schedule plastic surgery."

"No hospitals for me, thanks," Liana countered, still trying to adjust to the idea of visiting with so many people at one time. "I offered to stay in my room all night, but Mother wasn't the least bit receptive to the idea."

"Maybe we can stay on the fringe of things and disappear when everyone's busy eating," Jamie suggested.

"Jamie! Liana!" They were being called before their escape plans could even be finalized. Liana grimaced and moved closer to the largest cluster of people. Then she caught sight of the guest of honor, and her heart nearly skipped a beat.

Nate's eyes homed in on her the instant she left the shelter of the house, and Liana's eyes were immediately drawn to his compelling gaze. Her nerve endings leapt to alertness, and a potent electrical charge vibrated between them.

Only the most astute observer would have noticed the silent exchange, but Jamie apparently noted Liana's heightened color and tense posture. Her eyes questioned.

"Jamie, I don't think you've met our new neighbor," Liana commented as Nate separated from a group of guests and moved close to the two women. "This is Nate Harden. Nate, this is my best friend, Jamie Smith."

The openly admiring smile Nate gave Jamie brought faint color to her cheeks and sparkle to her eyes. They exchanged appreciative glances that made Liana uneasy.

"It's nice to meet you, Mr. Harden," Jamie greeted with a captivating smile and outstretched hand.

"Nate, please, and the pleasure is mine," he replied smoothly. "Forgive me if I refuse your hand, Jamie, but the doctor told me to keep my hands to myself," he apologized, raising hands that were lightly covered with gauze bandages.

A sickening feeling of dread washed over Liana and brought her eyes to his in shock. "Poison ivy." They proclaimed the damning diagnosis in unison.

Liana wanted to rip her tongue out of her mouth. Why had she confessed any knowledge of his condition? She swiftly averted her eyes, and silently implored Jamie not to comment on the subject.

Jamie's features displayed surprise and confusion as she looked from Liana to Nate and then back to Liana.

Nate's eyes registered curiosity, dawning comprehension, and then concern. He made a brief, thorough survey of Liana, but didn't see anything wrong.

His first thought was that she was more lovely every time he saw her. His second reaction was admiration for the loose-fitting gown that only hinted at the exquisite body beneath it. Then he put two and two together. His eyes glittered with unspeakable questions.

Color rose in Liana's cheeks, and Jamie cast her a confused glance. Turbulent blue eyes implored her friend not to ask any questions. A light touch on her arm announced Rod's arrival. She cursed his timing, but gave him a smile.

Unreasonable guilt prevented her from greeting Rod with her usual kiss and hug. "Rod, you've met Nate."

Rod started to extend a hand, but dropped his arm about Liana's shoulders when he noticed the bandages.

"The crew working on my pipeline said the ivy vines were thick at the pond, but the warning came a little late." Nate explained how he'd gotten his poison. "It's not bad, but I don't want to spread it to all the neighbors."

Liana was glad that no one pursued the subject. The men started discussing the benefits of piping artesian water to the house. She heaved a silent sigh of relief until she noticed that Nate's eyes were carefully scrutinizing her.

She knew he was mentally reviewing every inch of her body that his hands had touched, and sensual warmth engulfed her at the thought. She was greatly relieved when her father called him away to introduce him to more of their neighbors.

"What gives?" Rod asked, aware of the tension between Nate and Liana.

"Nothing where he's concerned." She tried to sound convincing. Rod and Jamie were both regarding her strangely, so she deliberately distracted them.

"Daddy was hoping you'd help him with the chef's duties tonight," she told Rod with forced cheerfulness. "Do you mind?"

"Nope. I'm pretty good at slinging hash," he teased. "Do I get a real chef's hat and apron?"

"No, but if you do a good job, you get your supper."

Rod grumbled good-naturedly and ambled toward the barbecue pit. Liana felt both relief and guilt. The relief only lasted until Jamie maneuvered her into the kitchen.

"What gives?" her friend demanded. "And don't play dumb. I know your hunk of a neighbor has poison on his hands, and you have it all . . . over . . . your . . . body!"

"It's not as interesting as it seems," Liana

hedged. "I must have gotten into poison ivy when I was swimming at the pond. I assume Nate did the same."

"That's it? That's all you're going to tell me?" Jamie exclaimed in disbelief. "If it's such an innocent coincidence, then why were sparks flying between the two of you? And why were his eyes smoldering while you turned three shades of red? Do I look like I was born yesterday?"

Liana had to laugh. Jamie had a knack for making her laugh even when she didn't want to. "One of these days I'll write my memoirs and give all the gory details."

"I suppose that means I have to mind my own business," Jamie complained. "You know how I hate that."

Liana laughed in genuine delight, and soon the two of them were in a party mood again. The subject of poison ivy was officially closed. Respect for privacy was important.

Jamie was like family, and she didn't hesitate to share the hostess duties. She and Liana visited with people they'd known all their lives, yet hadn't seen in years. They were kept busy, and the evening passed quickly.

Liana felt Nate's eyes on her many times during the next few hours. Each time he started in her direction, she involved herself in conversation with a large group of people. She didn't want to be alone with him. She didn't even like being so fiercely aware of him.

He looked incredibly handsome. Dressed in khaki slacks and a white cotton shirt, he was casually elegant, yet he radiated raw masculinity. Liana didn't think there was a woman present who remained unaffected by his magnetism.

She was no exception. His blond, bronzed image taunted her and forced her to remember the hard, smooth feel of his flesh. It was a challenge to keep her mind off the more intimate thoughts of how his big body felt against hers.

A small band was providing music, and once everyone had eaten, the patio was cleared for dancing. Japanese lanterns added a romantic touch as their guests became engrossed in one of their favorite pastimes.

Liana saw her dad motioning for her, and reluctantly skirted dancing couples to answer the silent summons. Nate was with Dave, and she didn't trust their benign smiles.

"Nate thinks he might know what's ailing our apple trees," her dad told her. "Why don't you take him out to the orchard and let him have a look?"

Liana's eyes narrowed, and she frowned at her father. What was he up to? Why did he want her to be alone with Nate? Her first impulse was to refuse, then an inexplicable feeling of protectiveness made her reconsider her response.

Instinct told her that Nate was reaching the limits of his patience. She could empathize with him. He'd been charming all evening, but she sensed the heightened tension in him. Being charming could take a toll on the nerves.

He didn't seem like much of a party animal, and she knew he was more than ready to escape the throng of curious people. She also realized he wouldn't be satisfied until he knew the details of her poisoned flesh.

It would be dark soon, and Nate couldn't get a good look at the trees, yet she accepted the sorry excuse to lead him away from the gathering.

"The orchard is on the other side of the barn," she said in an attempt to ease the ever-present tension between them.

Nate fell into step beside her and gently grasped her elbow with a bandaged hand. "Will we finally be alone and able to talk?" he asked.

Liana was acutely aware of his touch, the warmth radiating from his big body, and the disturbing heat of bedroom eyes trained exclusively on her. "We should be safe from interruption."

"Good," he murmured.

Liana didn't think there was anything good about it.

The sun was casting a final, glorious scarlet pattern across the western sky as it dipped below the horizon and allowed the climbing moon to take its rightful place as illuminator of the night. The sweet perfume of apple blossoms enveloped Nate and Liana as they entered the orchard. The evening began to take on an aura of romantic enchantment.

Feeling suddenly shy, Liana moved from Nate's side and leaned against the trunk of an apple tree. Her pose was unconsciously alluring, and her voice was unusually husky when she spoke.

"You won't be able to see anything tonight."

"I know," Nate admitted, moving very close to her. "I'll come back and check the trees another time."

Liana nodded. She'd known that her father's goose chase had nothing to do with apple trees. "So why are we here?"

Her head was tilted slightly upward to look into his eyes, and Nate slid a finger beneath her chin, stroking it gently. "You've been avoiding me tonight, nymph," he accused softly.

Liana's heart rate had increased slightly when Nate came near, but his touch made it pump overheated blood through her body at an alarming rate. She couldn't seem to tear her eyes from his even though she knew she could be rapidly hypnotized.

"I'm trying to be the perfect hostess," she defended, lowering her lashes to block the brilliance of his gaze. "You seem to be handling all the attention with ease." In fact, she knew he'd been charming everyone at the party, especially the women.

Nate withdrew his fingers and studied the delicate beauty of her face. No woman, however beautiful, had ever affected him as violently as this woman did. What she said about the party crowd was true. His business dealings had taught him how to socialize, yet he hated it.

He never felt completely comfortable when so many people were interested in him personally. He would have felt more at ease with Liana by his side.

"Am I being publicly punished for invading your privacy at the pond?" he asked in a light tone.

Liana's eyes flew to his. "You weren't the one who was trespassing, remember?" she teased.

Then, without considering the possible consequences of her actions, she began to rub her hot, itchy back against the rough bark of the tree. The itching had been driving her crazy all night!

Nate's grin was wicked and provocative. "So you have poison ivy on your back," he teased.

"I have it everywhere!" she charged. Then her breath caught in her throat when she glimpsed the swiftly concealed flare of desire in his eyes.

"Come here," he commanded softly.

There was barely a foot of space between them, yet Liana didn't budge an inch. Neither did she resist when he reached out and pulled her toward his hard, muscled body. The initial contact with his warmth was disquieting, but doubts were swiftly overcome by the unique pleasure Liana felt in his arms.

The smell and feel of him were dangerously potent. She knew she shouldn't allow him the slightest liberties, yet she couldn't find the strength to resist.

Slowly, and with infinite tenderness, Nate began to rub his bandaged hands over her irritated back, and all thoughts of resistance vanished. She'd been dying to scratch all evening, but hadn't dared alert anyone to her discomfort.

"Mother and Daddy will expect an explanation." Liana voiced her thoughts aloud, accompanying them with a heartfelt sigh.

"I took care of the explanations," Nate assured her. "I told your dad that I found poison ivy along our bordering fences. He decided you must have climbed through the vines when you took Smokey for a walk."

Liana nodded in acceptance of the explanation. It would suffice. Meanwhile, his hands were incredibly soothing. She arched closer to direct his touch to other areas of her backside. Nate willing obliged and widened the area of his massage.

His gentle caresses relieved their mutual irritation, but initiated a different kind of itch. Liana couldn't help but notice the increasing tempo of his heartbeat where her head rested against his chest. She knew she should do something to halt the aroused signals his body was transmitting to hers, but she didn't move out of his arms.

The gentle rubbing ceased as Nate clasped her more tightly against him, pulling her hips to his and making her aware of his masculine response to having her soft, pliant body close to his own. Liana's lashes fluttered open as she tilted her head and gazed at him with the same curious wonder she'd displayed the first time they met.

"I can't make any pretense about the depth of my desire for you," he told her gruffly as he lost himself in the slumberous brilliance of her eyes. "It's been two long days since I held you, and I'm not a patient man."

Liana was mesmerized by the passionate intensity of his expression and the rigid control she knew he was maintaining. He weakened her knees and crumbled her defenses with the tender urgency of his words.

The languid warmth stealing over her body and infiltrating her limbs left her with little resistance. When his lips sought hers, her heart stopped, and then renewed its beat with heavy pounding at every pulse point in her body. The kiss deepened and lengthened with a dizzying duel of tongues that made her feel hopelessly fragile, yet sensually powerful.

"You have the smallest, sweetest mouth I've ever tasted," whispered Nate, his tone rough and his mouth raining hungry kisses over her eyes, nose, and cheeks.

"I imagine that's either a bald-faced lie or a staggering compliment," Liana countered huskily.

"It's a compliment," Nate murmured as he caught her lips in another heart-stopping, wildly possessive kiss.

His hands started moving over her body with a seductive expertise that made Liana feel like melting, simply flowing to the ground with mindless movements. The responsiveness of her body alarmed her more than anything else might have done.

She gradually eased her lips from Nate's. "I think it's time we got back to the party." The breathy appeal in her tone revealed the depths of her responsiveness.

She wondered if she'd taken leave of her senses. Every time she was near Nate Harden, her body seemed to have a mind of its own. She wasn't pleased with the knowledge.

He eased his grip on her, but his eyes continued to hold her captive. "Are you worried about your reputation, or have you just remembered your boyfriend?"

"You are the guest of honor," she reminded, stepping from the circle of his arms. She didn't want to discuss Rod.

"We can tell everyone we're discussing business."

"Business?" Liana challenged, regaining a little spirit once she'd put some distance between them.

"Really," Nate assured her. He let her move out of his reach even though he clearly didn't want to. "That's the excuse I gave your dad."

"I wondered what the two of you had cooked up."

"I told your dad I had a proposition to make, and he gave me the okay. He came up with the apple tree blight all by himself."

"A proposition?" Liana was intrigued, but wary. He seemed entirely too pleased with himself. "I assume it's not immoral or illegal if Daddy approved."

"It's a perfectly respectable plan that popped into my mind while you were doing your best to avoid me this evening."

Liana's brows arched haughtily. "Okay, let's have it."

BEDROOM EYES

FIVE

Nate reached out a hand to brush an errant strand of hair off Liana's cheek. He studied her features in the shadowed haze of twilight. Her eyes were bright. Her cheeks were flushed with reaction to their embrace. Her lips were moist from his kisses.

Something stirred within him that had nothing to do with physical desire. He'd had the same stunned reaction the first time they'd met. He ached in ways he'd never experienced, and he wasn't sure how to handle the onslaught of emotions.

"The proposition?" Liana prompted, trying to dispel the web of intimacy he was creating with just his eyes.

"I'd like you to take charge of the redecorating of my house," Nate told her. "I haven't had time to interview decorators. Your dad says you're familiar with the house, and you have excellent taste. He said you're getting restless and want to work. Since you've promised to spend the summer at home, it would be a perfect solution to our problems."

Perfect. For a minute all Liana could do was stare at Nate in amazement. His mansion home was an historic landmark. She loved every inch of it. Even as a child she'd dreamed of ways to refurbish the stately house. She'd assumed the new owner would hire a team of professionals for the decorating.

"I didn't think the idea would shock you speechless," said Nate.

"What about your mother?" asked Liana. "Won't she want to help with the decorating or hire someone she's worked with in the past?"

"We both have ideas and preferences, but no firm plans for the overall project. It's a big place, and we'll need professional help."

"What work has already been done?" Liana couldn't hide her avid interest.

"The kitchen and a couple bedrooms were remodeled by a local firm. I've got carpenters doing general repairs, but the house is ready for wall covering, carpets, and furniture. I don't have the time to take care of all the details."

Liana knew she was being offered the career opportunity of a lifetime. The project was a decorator's dream. Still, she hesitated. Accepting the job meant working for Nate, and working with him on a daily basis.

"I'll pay you the going rate for New York designers. That's higher than most Ohio firms can offer, and you'll have a good-sized budget for the actual remodeling." He wasn't above using a little bribery.

"What size budget?" Liana found herself asking.

He quoted a price range that made her giddy with excitement. She didn't care much about her own fee, but she would love having a free hand at decorating his home without worrying about the cost.

"We'll have a straightforward contract with no strings attached?" she wanted to know.

Nate's eyes narrowed. "What kind of strings did you think I'd want to attach?"

Liana felt herself blushing again. It was annoying. "If I agree to work for you, I want our relationship to be strictly professional."

His laughter echoed between them. "If you think I'm going to agree to that, you're crazy. I'll respect your professionalism, but that won't stop me from wanting you in my arms. You're an incredibly desirable woman. Nothing between us is ever going to be strictly business."

"I think you're wrong," Liana argued.

She wanted to believe she could ignore her irrational physical responses to Nate while concentrating on her work. She didn't want him thinking she was an easy target, but every time he came close, she acted like a mindless idiot. She wanted some respect. It was suddenly very important to prove that she was a talented and capable professional. To do so, she'd have to stay out of his arms.

"I'll take the job on the condition that you keep your hands to yourself whenever we're working together. The first time you try to kiss me, I'll quit."

Nate didn't like being manipulated, and he didn't like conditions. He didn't want to keep his hands to himself, either. "Pretty damned arrogant, aren't you?" he taunted, watching her blush deepen. He already wanted her back in his arms.

"I love my work, and I'm very good at it. If I

lacked confidence in myself, I couldn't expect employers to have confidence in me, could I?''

"Are you just as certain that I'd have a hard time keeping my hands off you?'' he queried in a soft tone. ''Or are you afraid you might learn to like my kisses a little too much?''

"See!'' exclaimed Liana. ''I haven't even agreed to work for you, and you're already issuing sexual challenges. As much as I would love the job, I won't work under those conditions.''

Nate clamped his teeth shut. She was right. He couldn't force her to want him as much as he wanted her. He understood her concerns, but he had trouble thinking of her without having sexual urges.

"How about a compromise?'' he suggested. ''I promise I won't touch you while you're working in my house. That doesn't mean I won't respond to any advances you might make,'' he teased wickedly, "but I swear I won't ever harass you.''

"A strictly professional relationship?'' Liana wanted a firm commitment.

"During working hours,'' Nate clarified. ''I'm making no promises beyond that.''

Liana knew it was the best bargain she was going to get. It was all she needed to sway her decision. "I'd like to accept the position, providing my parents don't have a royal fit. I did promise to rest and recuperate.''

"I've already cleared it with them,'' he explained. "I promised not to let you work too hard or for too many hours. They agreed that you need a challenge to keep you from getting too bored and restless.''

"I'm pleased that everybody is happily arranging

my life for me," she retorted derisively. "It's just like being in grade school again."

Nate's smile was wide and wicked. He was tempted to pull her into his arms, but he didn't want her to change her mind about working for him.

Instead of reaching out a hand for her, Nate offered Liana his arm. She slipped a hand under his elbow, and he kept a tight grip while they headed back to the party.

Liana was amazed at how good it felt to be walking close to Nate; touching him, feeling his strength and warmth. She barely knew the man, yet he had a shocking impact on her senses. His very existence seemed to challenge her on every level. It was worrisome, but incredibly intriguing.

They were halfway back to the house when they caught sight of Rod and Jamie ahead of them. The other couple was moving hurriedly toward the patio and appeared to be arguing. Their actual words were indistinguishable, but their tones hinted at flaring tempers.

Liana frowned. She didn't resist when Nate pulled her closer to his side. "I wonder what's gotten into those two. Jamie acted strange this evening whenever I mentioned Rod. What could they be fighting about? They've always been the best of friends."

"Maybe their friendship is developing into something a lot more serious," Nate suggested smoothly.

Liana stopped and turned toward him, her eyes flashing. "What's that supposed to mean?"

"It means that he hasn't taken his eyes off her all evening," Nate said, refusing to release his hold on her hand. "While he watched her every move, Jamie was avoiding him as effectively as you avoided me."

Liana opened her mouth to protest and then closed it again. Had she been so worried about Nate that she'd totally missed the anger brewing between her friends? Why were they angry with each other? Was it just anger?

"What are you suggesting?" she asked.

"That your boyfriend has the hots for your best friend," Nate crudely informed her.

Liana was genuinely amazed by his assessment. Jamie had never hinted that she felt anything but friendship for Rod, and Rod had never treated Jamie with anything but affection. "Why would you think there's something going on between the two of them?"

"Because he has those hungry eyes when he looks at her," Nate replied. She tried to pull her hand from the crook of his arm, but he drew her fully against him and held her tightly.

"I recognize the hunger because I've been feeling it for a certain reluctant blonde," he added in a low tone. He dipped his head to brush a kiss over her pouting lips.

It was becoming a habit for Liana to lose her train of thought when Nate held her in his arms. It was a dangerous state of affairs. She knew it, but she couldn't seem to do anything about it.

"Kiss me," Nate murmured close to her ear.

A shiver raced over Liana at the husky tone of his demand. She felt the resurgence of tension in his big body, and knew she had to put a halt to this seduction of senses.

"No," Liana insisted firmly. She untangled herself from his arms and glared at him in the moonlight. "I don't want to play games with you. I know this is all a big game, but I'm not interested. You'll have to find some other local girl to entertain you.''

She was dead wrong. Nate wasn't playing games. In fact, he was out of his depths where she was concerned. The desire to hold her was the most natural reaction he'd ever had to any woman, but he didn't know how to explain so that Liana would believe him. He'd never been good at expressing his feelings with pretty words.

"I'm not looking for quick thrills, and I'm not a traveling salesman taking advantage of local women. I'm here to stay. The farm is my future, whether you believe it or not. You're determined to deny what's between us, but I'm being completely honest about the way I feel."

"Lustful," Liana taunted bravely.

Nate didn't deny it, but he knew there was a lot more than lust between them. Right now he wanted her to admit that it was foolish to cling to Rod.

"You're trying to hide behind a relationship that's lukewarm, at best. Rod treats you more like a sister than a lover." He didn't need to add that he'd have been murderous if Rod treated her any other way.

Liana felt her temper rising. Nate might be right, but he didn't have to be so damned smug about it. "It just so happens that Rod and I have never been lovers. Maybe that's where we've gone wrong. Maybe I should rectify the situation immediately."

With her threat hanging in the air between them, Liana swiftly headed for the noise and laughter at the house. She knew her declaration had shocked their sophisticated guest of honor, but she didn't care.

"Liana!" Nate's tone was a deep, dangerous

growl. He grabbed hold of her and swung her around to face him. "Don't threaten me!"

Her eyes sparkled with defiance. "What happens between Rod and me is none of your business."

"I'm making it my business," he bit out roughly. "Don't make love with him just to spite me."

Liana was feeling angry and spiteful. She glared at Nate in the dim light and jerked free of his arms. She wanted to walk away from him, but glimpsed a vulnerability in his eyes that deflated her anger and left her shaken. He really cared. Her careless threat had wounded more than his ego.

"You're driving me crazy!" she declared, shattering the heavy silence that followed their angry exchange. How could one man evoke so much physical and emotional chaos?

Their breathing was shallow and sounded as though they'd been running hard. Liana was trying to run, but Nate wouldn't let her. He wouldn't let her forget the way she felt when he held her close. It was totally out of character for her to melt in a man's arms, and she was confused by the chaotic state of her emotions.

"That makes us even," Nate assured her.

He'd been stunned to learn that she and Rod weren't lovers. For days he'd tortured himself with images of a reunion between Liana and her lifelong boyfriend. Seeing them together tonight had allayed the fears until she'd threatened to make love to Rod as an experiment in relationships.

"I suggest we return to the party and keep a safe distance between us the rest of the night," said Liana.

"Or maybe we could try making love and seeing

if that remedies the problem," came Nate's terse response.

Liana caught her breath. She forced herself not to fantasize about his hard body and hot kisses. She had to talk to Rod and sort out her feelings before she would be free to explore the tumult of emotions Nate generated.

"I need to talk to Rod."

"You need to tell him it's over."

Liana bristled at his tone. At the moment, Rod's undemanding attentions held great appeal.

"I don't need to be told what to do."

"Not as long as you remember that I'm the only man you need in your life," Nate argued, fear making his tone harsh and uncompromising.

"You'll be the only one if and when I say so," Liana countered furiously. "I don't even like you very well!"

In the space of a heartbeat she was slammed against his chest and trapped against his hard body with arms that gave her no slack. Nate's mouth was no longer gentle and coaxing. With this kiss he was demanding a response from her that couldn't be denied.

Liana whimpered and struggled, but to no avail. Her body liked the feel of him too much. Nate's ravenous hunger left her weak and trembling. No man had ever wanted her with so much primitive, undisguised need. The desire that rocked her body was foreign, frightening, and fascinating.

Nate felt the shudder rip through Liana and groaned into her mouth. When her arms slid over his chest, he made sure the two of them were hidden behind the barn. Then he clutched her tighter and pulled her soft curves against the tautness of his body. He was one big, throbbing ache.

She fit him perfectly. Her firm, unconfined breasts were crushed to his chest. He could feel the tightness of her nipples through their clothing and he wanted to taste her. The straps of her dress were no problem.

When his hot, searching mouth touched the curve of her breast, Liana gasped and clutched at handfuls of his hair. When his hungry mouth captured a nipple, she thought she would suffocate from pleasure. She couldn't catch her breath, and she didn't even recognize the low moans gurgling from her throat.

"Nate!"

He'd never heard anything so beautiful as the sound of her increasing excitement. He'd never tasted anything so satisfying as her sweet, tight nipples. He'd never been so aroused in his life. He was rapidly losing control. He wanted to lift her skirt and bury himself in her softness.

Liana was undulating her hips against the rigid evidence of his arousal. He was creating an ache deep within her that begged for satisfaction. She wanted him closer, and she wanted his mouth.

Nate managed to drag his lips from her breasts and satisfy the need for deeper, harder kisses. Their tongues dueled. They sucked at each other's mouths eagerly and without restraint.

A low, agonized groan escaped him as Liana caught fire in his arms. He wanted nothing more than to quench the fires and then stroke them to life again and again.

"Nate!" Liana cried again as she felt his bandaged hand caressing her thigh. When his roaming fingers rose higher, she dragged in a ragged breath and fought for control.

"Let me love you," he urged hoarsely.

His mouth found the sensitive curve of her neck while his hand sought a different curve of her body.

Liana's breathing was tortured, but at the feel of his intimate caress, she managed to pull herself together and let him know that she wanted him to stop.

"Please, Nate, I'm not ready for this."

"You're ready," he rasped huskily.

"Nate, please!"

He honored her plea with great difficulty. He'd never come so close to losing control. He'd never even come close to the edge. He was falling hard.

They both fought for breath. Collective laughter from the party was a stunning reminder of how reckless their passion had been. Liana moaned her displeasure with herself.

"I can't believe I'm making out behind the barn with a hundred people only yards away."

"Anytime, anywhere," Nate offered thickly. He was having more difficulty pulling himself together.

Liana made an effort to straighten her clothes and hair, but her hands were trembling and her whole body was quivering with aftershocks of passion.

Nate helped her as much as possible and smoothed her hair from her damp face. "You're mine." He couldn't resist the need to make her admit that they shared something special.

Liana stiffened at the words and stepped out of his reach. "Is that what this was all about?" she charged. "Was this your way of staking a claim so that I wouldn't throw myself at Rod?"

Yes and no, thought Nate, but he wasn't sure he

should voice his thoughts. Yes, he wanted her to know the extent of his desire and agree that they deserved a chance. He badly wanted to stake a claim.

No, he hadn't been thinking of Rod when he'd kissed and held her. He didn't want to use their love-making as an act of control. He wanted their relationship based on mutual need.

"I've been honest with you. I want you to be honest with me, Rod, and yourself."

Liana sighed deeply. She knew he was right. She'd always prided herself in being honest; even if it hurt. In this case, she was sure it would.

"I'll talk to Rod tonight. I'm not sure what I'm going to say, but I'll try to get some things sorted out."

Nate nodded, relieved. His hand was gentle as he pulled her against his side and began walking toward the house again.

"We'd better circle around to the front door," Liana said. "I'd like to brush my hair and repair my makeup before I face anyone."

"Good idea," Nate agreed.

Night had fallen and no one could see beyond the lights of the patio, so the two of them made their way to the front of the house unnoticed.

Their luck ran out on the front porch, where Rod was sitting alone in the swing. The light was bright, clearly illuminating Liana's tousled appearance. Rod's brows rose expressively as he took in the sight of the couple.

"Well, I'm sure batting a thousand tonight," he commented in self-derision. "Jamie won't have anything to do with me because of you, and you obviously don't give a damn what I do. That's two strikes. One more and I'm out. I wonder if there's an available female around who'd like to hear my sob story?''

Relief washed over Liana and drained some of her tension. She felt Nate relax, too. Rod wasn't angry or hurt by her defection.

''Maybe you shouldn't be so quick to give up on Jamie,'' she suggested lightly.

Rod just grunted in disgust. ''We need to talk,'' he told Liana.

Her eyes met Nate's. ''I'm going up to my room for a minute, and then Rod and I need a little privacy. You need to rejoin the party.''

Nate was a little slow to respond. He shot Rod a quick glance and then returned his steady gaze to Liana. ''I'll tell your folks that we've come to an agreement. That should explain our lengthy absence.''

Liana's smile was warm. ''Thanks.''

''I'll be right back,'' she told Rod as she and Nate moved into the house.

''I'll be here,'' he assured her.

It didn't take Liana long to repair the damages of her trip to the orchard with Nate. She hurriedly applied makeup and returned to the front porch. Rod hadn't moved. He reached out a hand for her as she joined him on the swing.

Liana grasped his hand with both of hers and brought it to her mouth for a kiss. ''I've loved you all my life, you know,'' she told him.

''And I've loved you,'' he replied, ''but I've recently found out that there's more to happily-ever-after than the kind of love we share.''

''Jamie?'' Liana asked.

''It struck like a bolt of lightning,'' Rod explained.

"When I got home, I went to her house and rolled her out of bed like I've always done. But this time it was different; really different."

Liana laughed lightly at his shocked tone. She should have felt jealousy or envy, but neither came. Rod and Jamie both held a special place in her heart. If love blossomed, she would dance at their wedding.

"How about you and Harden?" Rod asked. "You seem to be throwing caution to the wind. It's not like you."

"I don't seem to have much choice in the matter," Liana responded. "I've never met anyone who makes me feel the way Nate does. It's a little scary."

"Don't let him push you too hard or too fast."

Liana grinned at Rod's fierce tone. "He's pushy, all right," she admitted. "He's also very passionate, very tender, and sexy as hell. Despite all that, I trust him."

Rod roared with laughter and gave her a bear hug. "As long as you're being so practical and analytical, I won't worry too much," he teased.

Liana caught his face between her hands and gave him a loud, smacking kiss. "I love you," she declared lightly. "And don't you ever forget it."

"The feeling's mutual," said Rod.

Jamie chose that moment to step out the front door. Rod went rigid, and Liana quickly shifted away from him. She wanted to explain that they were officially ending their relationship, but Jamie didn't give her a chance.

"Sorry to interrupt," she told them, her tone carefully controlled. "It's getting late, and I'm heading home. I just wanted to say good night."

She was off the porch and moving quickly toward

her car before Rod and Liana could react. When they heard her car door slam and the engine roar to life, they both started swearing under their breaths.

"She's never going to forgive us," Liana moaned.

"She'll forgive you, just not me," said Rod.

"You'd better follow her and explain."

"You want me to die?" he asked grimly. "She had to hear us swearing eternal love to each other, and no matter what I say, she's going to think I'm a cheat and a liar."

"She won't think that."

"Wanna bet?"

"So find a way to convince her that she's wrong. Tell her that everything's over between us, and I'll be happy to confirm the fact."

"Forget it," Rod snapped, rising from the swing. "If she can't trust me to tell her the truth, then we don't have a future, anyway."

"Rod! Don't be that way! Jamie has every reason to be concerned. You and I have gone together for years. Everyone thinks we'll be getting married soon. You can't expect Jamie to offer her unconditional love if she believes you love me."

"Can't I?" he growled.

Liana groaned. Men! she thought. They could be so sweet and reasonable sometimes. But when it came to the women in their lives, they were totally irrational.

She couldn't coax Rod to follow Jamie or even call her, so they rejoined the party just in time to wish some of the guests a good night.

Liana had her doubts about how good a night it had been. Rod made her promise not to call Jamie, and she was torn between concern for her two best friends.

She carefully avoided Nate when they returned to the party, and she knew it made him angry. His tone was cool when he said his farewells.

"Thanks for everything," he told Dave and Gloria. To Liana he said, "I'll pick you up early on Monday morning."

"Not too early," Gloria insisted. "I know you're both anxious to get to work on the house, but Liana will have to take it easy awhile longer."

"You don't need to pick me up," Liana insisted.

"Sure he does," said Dave. "That way he can have breakfast while he's waiting for you."

Nate gave her father a smile, but his eyes were cooler when they shifted to Liana.

"How's eight o'clock?"

"Fine."

SIX

Nate's Greek-style mansion looked even more beautiful than Liana remembered. The house had been given a fresh coat of paint that enhanced its splendor in the bright morning sunlight.

Any lingering doubts she'd had about working with Nate vanished when she stepped through the front door. The atmosphere seemed to cloak her with warmth and welcome.

"I'd forgotten just how much I love this house," Liana commented as Nate ushered her through the main hall.

The elegant, winding staircase had been refurbished and shone from a recent varnishing that brought out the beauty of the natural wood grain. Off the foyer, each room was connected with spacious archways instead of doorways. The whole place was big and spacious, a decorator's dream.

"I like it, too," Nate told her. "Even though it's a white elephant, it's comfortable." He didn't fully understand his reaction to the house. He'd never had a home where he felt he belonged, so it was surprising that this house gave him such a feeling of permanency. He attributed it to his Greek ancestry.

Nate followed Liana as she wound her way through the downstairs rooms of the house. Carpenters and plumbers were at work, but most were completing their individual projects. Floors and walls were bare, yet ready to be finished and furnished.

"What do you think?" Nate asked as they entered the kitchen.

The big room had been decorated in glossy white with varying shades of yellow. Copper pans gleamed over the island cooking table. There was a small dinette table and a breakfast bar with stools. It was bright, cheerful, and full of modern appliances.

"I love it." Liana didn't hesitate to show her enthusiasm. "Who did the decorating in here?"

"It was a combined effort," said Nate. "Mom likes a yellow kitchen, I liked the breakfast bar, and a lady at the paint store in town told me the island was a must if I wanted a fashionable kitchen."

Liana smiled. "Well, the finished product is perfect. What other rooms have you done?"

"My office," Nate said, leading her from the kitchen to a smaller room tucked beneath the staircase. It was paneled in dark wood. The old, built-in bookshelves had been replaced with sturdier boards, and the marble fireplace had been refurbished. The only furniture was a big desk and a couple of easy chairs.

"Mr. Drenasis used this as a library," Liana commented. "Did all his books sell at auction?"

Nate didn't answer her question, but asked one. "How well did you know the old man?"

Liana wondered at the strange tone of his voice and his disrespect for a deceased man. She replied with another question. "Did you ever meet Mr. Drenasis?"

"No." Nate didn't elaborate, and his tone didn't invite further questions.

"It's been years since I was here," Liana explained. "I came a lot as a teenager, but college and my career put an end to regular visits. Mr. Drenasis was a widower with no family in this country. I think he was a very lonely man."

Nate made a rough, derisive sound and then held the door for Liana to precede him from the office. She gave him a quick glance, wondering what had upset him, but she didn't ask. His earlier good humor seemed to have vanished.

"Where to next?" she inquired as she started down the hall toward the front of the house.

"I've had three bedrooms on the second floor redone. "You can take a look at them and check the others. I'm more worried about getting the downstairs finished, so you can leave the guest rooms for last."

They climbed the winding staircase slowly, because Liana was running her hands over the railing and stopping ever few stairs to survey everything around her.

"Do you have any specific decorating ideas yet?" asked Nate.

"Oh, yes!" she exclaimed, then calmed her tone. "Unless you want to go with all period items, I've always thought this house would be perfect for a blend of old and new. Some of the rooms beg for antique pieces, but you'll need comfort if you want it to be a home, not just a showplace.''

"I want a home.''

"Good.''

"The master bedroom is to the right of the stairs and overlooks the front of the house,'' Nate explained as he guided her toward his bedroom. "Are you familiar with all the rooms on this floor?''

"No,'' replied Liana. "Most of my visits were restricted to the downstairs rooms.''

He pushed open the door to his room, and she stepped just inside the door, immediately realizing that he used the master bedroom.

She couldn't fault the decor here, either. The room was done in an intriguing blend of blues and purple. A king-sized bed occupied one side of the room. There was another refurbished marble fireplace, a huge sliding-door closet, and the two dressers were polished to a high shine.

The only thing that bothered Liana was the slightly rumpled bedclothes. She had a sudden vision of Nate sprawled in the big bed, and a quiver of excitement caught her by surprise.

"I'm not much for making beds,'' he said. "I did throw the spread over it on your behalf this morning.''

"That was thoughtful,'' she replied, determined to keep her tone light. "Do you have a connecting bathroom?''

Nate swung the door to the bathroom open, and she peeked inside, but didn't go in. It was far too intimate. The room was still damp from his morning shower, and smelled of his cologne. Liana found it sensually disturbing.

"The other rooms?" she asked as she quickly backed away from him and moved toward the hallway door.

"What's wrong?" asked Nate as he followed her. "You act agitated, and I've been on my best behavior. Do you hate what I've done in here?"

"The bedroom is absolutely gorgeous," Liana admitted. It was just a little too masculine and too inviting for her peace of mind. "I'm just impatient to see the whole house."

Nate accepted her explanation and showed her through the other five rooms of the second floor. Three of them were yet to be finished. His mother had suggested the color and styles for the remaining two.

"Mom chose the rose shade for her room and green for Peter's room. Most of their furniture was shipped from New York."

"Who's Peter?"

"My cousin, Peter Harden. Mom and I are the only family he has. He worked for me in New York, but quit when I sold the hotels. Mom supports him most of the time. He's charming, easygoing, and good company for her."

"So he's going to be living here, too?"

"He's going to try," said Nate with a grin. "He was raised on a farm, but he's a city boy at heart. I give him about a month before he's climbing the walls."

Liana grinned. "You don't think our fair town will appeal to him?" she teased.

Nate sobered a little as he studied Liana. Her hair was pulled into a knot at her nape, enhancing the perfection of her features and the inviting curve of her neckline.

Her eyes were alight with laughter. The dress she wore was conservative in styling, but didn't conceal her generous feminine attributes. She had a special kind of appeal, and she would definitely appeal to his cousin Peter. He frowned at the thought. Why hadn't he considered that probability?

"Earth to Nate," Liana teased lightly. "I didn't know my question would send you into a trance."

Nate flashed her a grin. "You'll have to form your own opinion of Peter after you meet him."

"When might that be?" Liana asked as they finished their tour of the second floor, checking bathrooms and closets.

"Soon. They're coming sometime this week to take a look at the house. Right now they're staying with a friend of Mom's who's getting married in a couple weeks, so they won't be moving out here until July."

"Will this be the first time your mother has seen the house?"

Nate's eyes narrowed, and he acted as though her question were offensive. Liana couldn't imagine why such an innocent query would antagonize him, but he avoided a straight answer with another question.

"How much have your parents told you about my mother?" Nate asked warily.

"Only that she grew up in this area and was a friend of my mother's. I suppose she remembers this house even if she never visited here."

"She remembers it well," was Nate's only response. "But it's been almost thirty-five years since she saw it. Are you ready to head back downstairs?'' he asked, putting an abrupt end to the subject.

"I've always been curious about the third story of this house. Do you mind if I go up and have a look?''

"It's dirty up there,'' Nate told her, continuing to frown. "It's full of junk that belonged to the old man. It didn't sell with his other things, and I haven't had time to clean it out yet.''

"I love old junk,'' Liana insisted, glancing toward the door she knew led to another staircase. "If I'm keeping you from anything important, I'll be happy to continue my tour alone. After I've finished, we can set up a time to go over room dimensions, color charts, and some of your personal preferences.''

Nate leaned against the wall, crossed his arms over his chest, and stared at her with unflinching eyes. "That sounds very much like a brush-off.''

Liana slowly walked to the stairway door, leaned against it, crossed her arms over her chest, and returned his steady regard.

"I spent most of my teenage years dying with curiosity about the upper levels of this house. Now that I finally have the opportunity to satisfy that curiosity, you want to rain on my parade.''

Nate couldn't control the grin that tugged at his lips. She pouted so beautifully. He wanted to kiss her sassy mouth, but he'd promised to behave.

"You're pretty pushy, aren't you?'' he taunted, his eyes gleaming wickedly.

"Saturday night you called me arrogant,'' Liana reminded. "I figure it takes one to know one, and as a fellow arrogant, you should understand how I feel.''

"Do you always get what you want, Ms. Banner?"

"Do you always get what you want, Mr. Harden?"

Right at the moment he wanted her in his arms, with her warm, womanly body pressed close to his own. His muscles tightened at the thought. His bedroom was just a few steps from them. The desire to carry her to his bed was shocking in its intensity.

"I'll go upstairs with you," Nate conceded roughly.

It was an effort to breathe. Something in the look he was giving her set Liana's heart pounding erratically. So far he'd kept his promise, but for an instant his eyes had been dark with seduction. They made her think of bedrooms; one blue and purple bedroom in particular.

Reaching for the door behind her, Liana turned and quickly found a light switch for the stairway. Then Nate gently shoved her out of his way.

"I'd better go first. The electricians replaced all the wiring up here, but I haven't had time to look for other possible hazards."

The stairs were narrow, and the staircase was steep. The stairwell was boxed in on both sides, but well lit. Liana followed Nate, and was glad he ran into all the spider webs before she did.

When they stepped onto the upper floor, there was abundant sunshine coming through windows from all sides of the long, one-room attic.

"Nate, this would make a perfect studio or workroom. You could convert it to a billiard room, a playroom, or an exercise gym. That's what most people are doing with spacious old houses these days. With all this natural light, it would be great for a solarium, too."

"Only in the summer," he pointed out dryly.

"I guess it would cost a fortune to heat this floor all winter," Liana conceded. "It just seems such a shame not to make use of it."

"I won't be making full use of the rest of the house, so I'm not going to worry about this floor for anything but storage."

"It could be converted to an apartment if you ever decide to hire live-in employees."

Nate was shaking his head negatively, and Liana grinned. "If you ever get hard up for cash, you could rent it out to boarders," she teased.

"I'll keep that in mind," he declared with an answering grin. "Now are you satisfied enough to go back downstairs?"

Liana swept another glance around the room. All the old furniture had been pushed to the center of the room and covered with sheets of plastic.

"I haven't had a chance to explore," she replied. There was nothing so tempting as the treasures in an attic.

"Curiosity again?" Nate wanted to know.

"Do you mind if I peek under the plastic?"

He started shaking his head, both in exasperation and response to her query. Grabbing one end of the sheet of plastic, he peeled it from the collection of furniture that stretched the length of the room.

Liana gasped at the unveiling of more treasures than she could have ever imagined. "Oh!" she squealed in excitement. "A marble-topped washstand. A glass-topped tea trolley. Cane-bottom rocking chairs. They're at least a hundred years old!"

Her excitement increased as she moved around the furniture and carefully inspected each piece. Some were upside down, and some taller pieces were lying on their side.

"Nate, there's a complete dining room set here: a walnut table with four, six, eight chairs," she counted. "They're not even damaged, and there's a matching china hutch. Here's a hall tree, and there are several paintings," Liana exclaimed in delight.

"You're going to get filthy," Nate warned.

The total lack of enthusiasm in his tone made Liana momentarily abandon her exploration and spear him with a look of amazement. "Aren't you the least bit interested? This all belongs to you, and every piece is rare and valuable."

"I'll have to take your word for it. It just looks like dusty old junk to me."

"Junk!" Liana was aghast. She couldn't believe he wasn't interested. If he didn't like the antiques, he should at least be impressed with the fortune they were worth.

She shifted a few smaller pieces to get a better look at the dining room set. The table legs had intricate carvings that matched the carvings on the china cupboard and the backs of the chairs. Everything looked sturdy and well preserved.

"This will be absolutely perfect for the formal dining room downstairs," she told Nate, mentally picking complementary colors to highlight the beauty of the furniture.

"No."

Another glance at Nate confirmed her impression that he was serious. His expression was grim, and he viewed the furniture with contempt.

"No, what?"

"No, I don't want any of it used in my house.

You can have anything you want. You can give it away, sell it, or trash it, for all I care, but I won't use it. I'd rather see it all burned.''

Liana's mouth opened in amazement. She couldn't believe what she was hearing. How could he have such a strong dislike of such a wide variety of items?

''I thought you wanted me to incorporate a few antiques in your overall decor,'' she said.

''You can buy all the antiques you want,'' he countered. ''I just don't want any of this.''

Liana ran a hand over the solid wood frame of an old painting. ''Do you mind if I ask why?''

''Yes, I mind.'' Nate's reply was succinct, his tone firm.

Liana felt as if he'd slammed a door in her face. She looked directly at him, but found only harshness in his features. She was surprised at how much his attitude hurt, and she didn't have a clue to his feelings.

Dragging her gaze from his tight-lipped expression, Liana focused her attention on the painting at her feet. She lifted it slowly, and caught her breath at the signature. The now famous portrait artist had been dead for over thirty years, but his work was being shown in the finest galleries of the world.

Liana didn't bother to mention the fact to Nate. She had a feeling he wouldn't care. He was impatient to be out of the attic, but she couldn't resist studying the portrait.

The artist had captured all the vitality and enthusiasm of youth in the painting of a beautiful girl who looked to be in her late teens. She had dark, expressive eyes and hair as black as night. There was a hint of mischief in her eyes.

Liana momentarily forgot Nate's lack of enthusiasm and turned the canvas so that he could see the young woman. "Look at this," she whispered in awe. "She's beautiful, and the artist has captured a wealth of personality."

Nate took a step closer, and Liana was pleased that something actually interested him.

"By the looks of the dress she's wearing, this must have been painted about the time my mother was in high school. I've seen similar styles in her photo albums," Liana explained. "I wonder who she is."

Nate took the portrait from her and held it to the light, studying it intently. "She's my mother," he stated quietly.

"Your mother?" Liana repeated in surprise. "But she's so dark."

"A fluke of genetics," Nate replied.

"She also looks very Greek."

"She is very Greek."

Liana was thoroughly confused, but wanted to understand. "Was she a relative of Mr. Drenasis?"

Nate's expression tightened again. "She's his daughter," he told her in a clipped tone.

Liana's eyes flew back to the painting. Mr. Drenasis had been elderly and white-haired when she knew him. It was impossible to compare memories of him with the image of the woman in the portrait.

"But that makes you . . ."

"A bastard," Nate said curtly, his handsome features tight with emotion. "My mother was unfortunate enough to get pregnant out of wedlock at a time when that meant family shame and social disgrace."

Liana had a feeling that being conceived out of

wedlock concerned Nate more than it would most people. She was interested in his Greek heritage.

"You're Mr. Drenasis's grandson?"

"I'm not proud of the fact," growled Nate.

"But they said he didn't have any heirs," Liana insisted, trying to piece together the puzzle. "I know they couldn't have sold his property without checking all the public records and trying to track down relatives."

"The old man disowned my mother. He told her she'd be disinherited, and made sure she was by paying some local authorities to sign a death certificate with her name on it. He even bought a burial plot and gravestone. That's what the investigators would have found."

Liana was horrified, yet she didn't doubt that Nate was telling the truth. She stared at him with wide eyes. "That's terrible! How could anyone fake the death of their own child!"

"He did it," snapped Nate. "Worse than that, he threatened to destroy my real father's family if my mother didn't agree to marry one of his cronies."

"He forced her to marry someone else?"

"Yeah," Nate bit out, turning to set the portrait against a wall.

Liana realized that he wasn't going to offer any further information, and she didn't want to annoy him with probing questions. Still, she couldn't accept the fact that he'd probably just paid a small fortune for property that he should have inherited.

"Nate," she said hesitantly, "everything here belongs to you and your mother: the farm, the house, this furniture. Why did you buy it all? Your mother could go to court to prove her parentage and probably prove that the public records were forged.''

Nate's expression was cool and remote when he turned back to her. "She didn't want anything from the old man, and neither did I. She wanted to come home without causing another scandal, so I bought the place.''

Liana could understand a desire to return with as little fuss as possible, but there was bound to be gossip. "All the longtime residents of Springdale will remember your mother and probably drive her crazy with the same questions I've been asking.''

"She's prepared to be a ten-day wonder. She's tough, and she can handle the gossip. She just didn't want a court case that would stir up a lot of trouble and pain.''

Liana's next questions would have been about his natural father. Was he still a resident of Springdale? Was he a respected citizen of the community? Did he have a family of his own? Nate's tense demeanor and closed expression kept her from asking.

"Let's go downstairs,'' he said, his tone clipped. "It's hotter than hell up here.''

Liana's dress was clinging to her damp skin. The rest of the house had been comfortably cool, but the attic was hot and stuffy.

Nate started down the stairs, holding both arms to the walls of the narrow staircase to protect Liana should she stumble on the steep descent.

Liana clung to the iron railing as she carefully followed him. She stopped when he reached for the doorknob and turned it sharply to the left, then the right, with no results.

"What the hell?'' muttered Nate, turning the knob

more forcefully, then pounding on the door to see if it was stuck.

"What's wrong?" asked Liana.

"It's locked."

"Locked? Did I do something wrong when I closed it?"

"These old doors have skeleton keys. You couldn't have done anything."

"Well, the key didn't turn itself."

Nate's expression was grim as he turned to Liana. "There wasn't a key in the door. I put all the skeleton keys in a drawer in the kitchen."

Liana was suddenly very, very warm. Nate was standing two narrow steps down from her, and she was practically standing on top of him. The air was thin and hot, making breathing difficult for her.

"Are you suggesting that someone deliberately locked us in here?"

SEVEN

Nate's features tightened, and his eyes were cold. He didn't know why anyone would lock them in the attic, but he didn't like it. There had been other small, inexplicable incidents lately. Now he was sure someone was trying to sabotage the restoration of the house.

"Nate?"

He tilted his head to look up at Liana. He gazed into her confused eyes and attempted to control his anger. "It won't do any good to yell for help. There's too much noise downstairs," he explained. "We'll have to go back up to the attic and try to open a window."

Liana reached a hand to his shoulder, intending to support herself as she turned, but the feel of his muscled warmth momentarily distracted her.

She was so close that Nate could smell the musky sweetness of her perfume. Her touch caused a tremor deep in his body, and the heat of her hand singed his nerve endings. He wanted to wrap his arms around her and hold her close, but he'd promised not to pressure her while she was working in his house. He lifted his hands to her waist.

Liana put her other hand on his other shoulder. Her eyes were locked with his in a sensually questioning gaze. She was silently asking him if he felt the attraction as strongly as she did.

"You're playing with fire, Ms. Banner," Nate warned.

Liana knew he was right. She knew he wasn't going to break his promise unless she provoked him. She also knew she should be professional, not provocative; yet something about him tempted her as no other man had ever done.

Nate took one step closer, but Liana didn't retreat. Her arms slid around his neck, and his arms tightened about her waist.

"I just want a kiss," she told him lightly. "Just a kiss, nothing else."

Nate's breath caught in his throat. "You're making the rules. Take whatever you want."

Liana closed her eyes, and her mouth settled lightly on his. Their lips met in a gentle exploration that was slow, and sweet, and sexy.

She shifted her head slightly for a more thorough study of his lips. Nate murmured his approval of her investigation, and the movement of his lips encouraged Liana to slip her tongue into his mouth. He welcomed it warmly and wetly, tenderly stroking it with his own tongue.

Their lips pressed tightly together, and the full length of Liana's body swayed more fully towards Nate. He hugged her close, but kept his hands safely locked behind her back. He didn't want to do anything that would demean or discourage her sweet, spontaneous responses to him.

Liana was elated by the tenderness of their kisses. She withdrew her tongue and coaxed Nate's into her mouth, where she adored it as thoroughly as he had hers. The taste of him sent quivers of longing through her.

The tight space between the narrow stairwell walls soon became a breathless cocoon. The next time Liana was forced to drag in air, she drew back slightly and gazed at Nate with eyes full of turbulent emotion.

He was struggling to control his breathing, too. She was gorgeous, and he wanted all the sweetness she was capable of giving, but he didn't want pity.

"I hope this isn't a show of sympathy for the poor bastard who lost his inheritance," Nate challenged roughly. Liana eased away from him, sliding her hands to his shoulders and locking gazes.

"You don't strike me as a man who needs anyone's sympathy," she declared, her voice still husky from his kisses.

"Good," said Nate. He decided to put an end to the tender embrace before it could escalate into uncontrollable passion. His hands tightened at Liana's waist, and he gently urged her to turn around and precede him up the stairs again.

She quickly retraced her steps, conscious of the heat from his guiding hands. Her bold demand for a kiss left her feeling slightly embarrassed, but she was relieved that Nate didn't make any comment.

He moved to one of the windows facing the front of the house, but didn't see anyone he could call to.

Moving to the windows facing the back of the house, he caught sight of his farm manager, Ned Larkin. One of the window frames had been replaced recently, so it was easy to open.

"Ned!" Nate called from the window. "Ned!" he yelled louder until the other man heard him and shot a glance toward the upper level of the house.

Liana stood beside Nate and looked down on the manager. He was a tall, wiry man who never looked as if he got enough to eat. She remembered him from her visits to Mr. Drenasis, but she'd never really gotten to know him.

Nate explained their situation to Ned and asked him to find a key for the stairway door. Then he closed and locked the window before turning his attention back to her.

"You look hot and tired," he said. "Your parents will want you to quit working after the first day."

Liana was feeling the heat and humidity. It annoyed her that she still tired so easily, and that the heat zapped her strength. Her sophisticated chignon was drooping, with more tendrils of hair escaping than staying confined. Her lightweight dress was clinging uncomfortably, and she tugged at the fabric.

"It's hot everywhere," she grumbled.

"And you've done too much today, haven't you?" Nate asked quietly.

"I haven't done anything!" Liana groused. "It's barely past noon."

Nate grinned at her belligerent expression, but understood her frustration. He was always impatient with restrictions, and he knew how hard it was to slow down.

"As soon as Ned rescues us, we can have something cold to drink and rest while you explain your ideas for redecorating.''

Liana returned his grin, knowing that he understood her restlessness. ''Are you sure Ned will rescue us? He never was very fond of me.''

''Why do you say that?'' asked Nate as he pulled a chair from the pile of furniture. He dusted it with a handkerchief and shoved it toward Liana.

''I don't know,'' she replied as she sat on the chair. ''He was always polite, but I still got the impression that he didn't approve of my visits here.''

''He doesn't own the place and never has.''

''He's been in charge of the farm for as long as I can remember,'' reminded Liana.

''He's been here about twenty years,'' Nate explained. ''He stayed on as caretaker for the estate after the old man died. I hired him because he knows the farm better than anyone else in the area.''

''Dad says he really knows farming,'' added Liana. She continued to tug at the neckline of her dress, hoping to stir up a little breeze and cool her overheated flesh.

Nate's eyes followed the movement of the fabric against her breasts. It was a pity that they were confined beneath so much fabric, he thought. The memory of her lush, naked breasts had cost him hours of sleep the last two nights. The taste of her flesh also lingered in his memory, as did the feel of her responsive nipples in his mouth.

The images he conjured created a familiar ache. Nate felt his body's involuntary response to the memories, and swiftly forced his thoughts elsewhere.

''I think I hear Ned. Stay put until I'm sure he can get the door unlocked.''

Liana obeyed without argument. She needed a brief respite from the fire his eyes had been kindling within her. She couldn't remember ever being aroused by nothing more than a man's eyes on her. Nate Harden's eyes should be classified as armed and dangerous.

"Liana! Come on down," Nate called as he retraced his steps up the stairs to offer her a hand.

She grasped his hand and slowly descended the stairs. It was a relief to step into the second-story hallway. The temperature was a good twenty degrees cooler. She offered a smile and thank you to Ned.

"Miss Liana, it's good to see you again." The farm manager greeted her with a nod. "You look a little flushed. I hope you're feelin' okay. I heard you been sickly."

"I'm fine, thanks, just hot."

"How'd you come to be locked in the attic?" Ned's question was directed at Nate.

"I don't know. Where did you find a key?"

"I got one out of the kitchen where you put 'em," Ned explained, handing two keys to Nate. "But there was one layin' on the floor in front of the door."

Nate frowned and pocketed the keys. "It must have fallen out of the lock. Thanks for helping."

"No problem," said Ned. "You need anything else right now?"

"No. Liana and I are going to take a break. I'll have one of the carpenters take care of the locks up here."

"Miss Liana, you take care. Tell your mom and dad I said hello."

"Thank you, Ned. I'll do that."

The other man headed down the stairs. Liana knew

he was in his sixties, but he was quick and sure-footed. He'd been extremely nice.

"I don't suppose I look too professional at the moment, do I?" Liana asked. She tried to straighten her drooping chignon, but she knew she looked as hot and dusty as she felt.

Nate grinned. She looked beautiful to him, but her sophisticated facade was badly rumpled.

"I don't think any of the workmen downstairs are going to complain."

Liana sighed and headed for the stairs. She knew he was getting a kick out of the deterioration of her professional dignity. There didn't seem to be anything she could do about it.

Nate followed her down the stairs. As they headed from the front hall to the kitchen, the house grew quiet except for low murmurs from the carpenters. The construction crew was breaking for lunch.

Bill Matias, the crew foreman, stepped into the hallway from the living room. His eyes lit with pleasure when he spotted Liana.

"Bill!" she exclaimed when she recognized her high school classmate. He'd been president of her senior class and halfback for the school football team. He still looked as good as he had in high school. "It's been a while."

"Too long," he agreed with a grin. "I heard you were home, but didn't know you were out and about. Your mom says you're supposed to be convalescing."

Liana groaned, and Bill laughed. Then he shot a glance at Nate. "Is Liana the decorator you hired to finish the house?"

"Yes. She's just looking today, but she'll be giv-ing the orders from now on," Nate explained, his tone cool. He didn't like the way the foreman was looking at Liana. "She's supposed to take it slow."

"Nate, you're almost as bad as my mother," Liana admonished. "I'm not an invalid."

"You just tire easily?" he taunted.

"It's this damned weather," she argued.

"Better not let Gloria hear you swearing," Bill teased. "I can still remember the lecture she gave me when I said a nasty word in front of the cheerleading squad."

"As I recall, you were a little upset at the time."

"Sally was giving me fits. Sally's still giving me fits," he said, his tone growing more serious.

Sally was his childhood sweetheart. She and Liana were cheerleaders together for four years of high school. Bill and Sally had married the day after graduation.

"How is she?" Liana asked.

Bill shrugged. "I don't really know. We're separated and considering a divorce."

"Oh, Bill, I'm sorry to hear that. The two of you always seemed so perfect for each other. What happened to all those plans to increase the population of Springdale?"

"Not one new resident," Bill joked, but Liana had a feeling he was sensitive about the issue. He quickly changed the subject. "What about you and Rod? Are you finally going to announce a wedding date?"

Liana felt Nate stiffen. They'd never discussed what had transpired between her and Rod. She knew he was as interested in her response as Bill.

"Rod and I finally decided that there will never be wedding bells for us," she explained. "I hope we'll always be the best of friends, but marriage isn't in the picture.''

"No kidding?'' Bill didn't hide his surprise. "Does that mean you're officially available? That'll please the entire male population of this town.''

Nate groaned at the thought. His hold on her arm tightened, and he gave her a look that spoke volumes. The only male attention he wanted directed her way was his own.

Liana didn't realize how intimate her smile was as she shifted her eyes to Nate. "I'm not really interested in the male population of Springdale right now,'' she declared.

When her eyes shifted back to Bill, she saw a fleeting expression in his eyes that she found hard to identify. It was a strange mixture of envy and resentment. Someone called to him, and he excused himself with a friendly warning for her to take care of herself.

"I have a feeling that you and Rod will be the main topic of conversation for the whole town tonight,'' said Nate as he steered her toward the kitchen.

"The grapevine has always been awesome,'' Liana admitted. "You'll probably be labeled the outside influence.''

"I hope I am an influence,'' he said. "What would you like to drink? I have beer, milk, or water.''

"What exciting choices,'' she drawled, grinning. "I just don't know how I can decide.''

"You can have milk,'' Nate decided for her. "Your dad is a dairy farmer, and you need nutrition.''

"What if I don't like milk?''

"Tough." Nate poured her a tall glass of milk and brought it to the table.

Liana laughed. She was getting an enormous amount of pleasure from sharing time with Nate. Maybe it was just due to her weeks of forced convalescence.

Nate was getting addicted to her laughter. It was risky, but he couldn't seem to help himself. He popped the top off of a beer and took a long swallow. "Rest for a few minutes, and then I'll take you home."

"No. I have too much to do," Liana argued. "I want to get window and floor measurements for each room, and then we need to go over some color charts."

"Not today." Nate's tone was firm. "You'll have plenty of time to do everything, but I want you to keep the pace slow."

"I'm tired of slow!" Liana insisted heatedly.

"You're tired, period."

She knew he was right, but she didn't like it. "I hope you don't plan to fill in for my mother and dad with the nagging," she snapped.

"I promised them."

Liana heaved a sigh of defeat. Nate could prove to be more of a problem than her parents. They finished their drinks in silence.

"Are you ready to go?" he asked shortly.

Liana walked to the sink and rinsed her glass. "Ready," she replied flatly. "Let's go."

A step into the sunshine drained what was left of Liana's energy. Nate's pickup truck was like an oven when they climbed into it. As he noticed the effect the heat had on her, he swiftly apologized.

"Sorry, there's no air-conditioner in this truck," he explained. "Do you want to wait in the house while I get the car?"

"That's silly," Liana argued. "I won't melt before we get to my house." At least she hoped she wouldn't.

When they were moving, Nate turned on the fan to get air circulating in the cab. Neither of them spoke as they traveled the two miles between their homes. He dropped Liana off at her front door with a promise to pick her up at eight the next morning.

The next two weeks passed in a similar pattern. Some days they worked together at Nate's house, and other days they went shopping for home furnishings. They both helped supervise painting, wallpapering, and curtain hanging.

Nate never let Liana work a full eight-hour day, but she was happy to be doing the work she loved. She still tired too easily, and that frustrated her, but she blamed the continued heat for some of her weariness.

Liana had hoped that working with Nate every day would neutralize the attraction between them, but it did just the opposite. The sexual tension intensified.

They worked well together, and were careful not to initiate any unnecessary physical contact, but it didn't alleviate their acute awareness of each other. Their determination to ignore the attraction just made it worse.

Every time Nate's body brushed against Liana's, she felt a thrill of pleasure. Anytime they were close to each other, her breathing grew shallow, and her senses greedily absorbed the scent and feel of him.

Nate kept his promise to treat her as a professional when she worked in his home, but it was one of the hardest things he'd ever done. By the end of the second week, his fingers itched to tangle in her hair, his mouth ached for the taste of hers, his whole body quaked with repressed longings.

He'd hoped that Liana would take the initiative and put an end to their platonic relationship. She didn't, and he'd given his word to behave. It was killing him. He hadn't had a good night's sleep since the party, and the strain was wearing heavily on his nerves. Seeing her every day and not being able to touch her was a slow kind of torture.

Friday was especially hectic at the end of their second week of work. Carpet was laid in several rooms, and furniture was delivered throughout the day. Nate knew Liana was overexerting herself, but he didn't get her out of his house until late afternoon.

He drove Liana home in his BMW. The pickup truck was the standard mode of transportation on the farm, but he wanted to assure her comfort with the car's air conditioning.

She looked like a lovely, wilted flower, and he cursed himself for letting her do too much again. She just didn't have any low gear. She never moved slowly. She never sat still for more than a few minutes.

"You don't have any common sense when it comes to your health, do you?" he asked as he drove the distance between their homes.

Liana brushed straying strands of hair off her forehead. She'd been trying to pace herself, but she didn't have much experience in the art.

"I'm used to working sixteen-hour days," she explained. "Once I start a project, I'm impatient to see the final results. It seems like I'm working at a snail's pace now, but I still get tired so quickly."

"You get too tired too fast because you work at a hummingbird's speed," said Nate.

"Look who's talking," she countered. "You're always one step ahead of me. You make me come home and then go straight back to your house and put in more hours."

"It's my house. When I'm tired, I can relax."

"And how often do you do that?" she taunted. Nate was looking as tired and drawn as she felt.

He didn't respond. When he tried to relax, he thought of her, and his restlessness increased. He had to keep pushing himself right now.

As they turned in Liana's driveway, she was surprised to see a variety of unfamiliar vehicles parked near the house. "Mother must have planned another party without telling me," she said as Nate parked the car and shut off the ignition. "Would you like to come in for a minute?"

He nodded, climbed from the car, and joined Liana on the passenger side. Voices could be heard from the barnyard as they approached the porch. "Let's go see what's happening," she suggested.

They rounded the building and headed for the barn. The voices grew louder, and the overall tone was grim. Liana and Nate shared a questioning glance, then came to an abrupt halt as they rounded the barn.

"Oh my God!" Liana cried at the sight of the pasture.

Cows were down everywhere. The pasture was littered with sick dairy cows. A few of her dad's herd still stood on all four legs, but they were swaying unsteadily and looked ready to drop. Liana had never seen anything like it.

"Daddy!" she called to gain Dave's attention. She and Nate moved closer to the group of men standing over one cow. She recognized neighboring dairy farmers and the local vet. "What in the world is happening?"

Dave's expression was strained. "That's what we're trying to find out," he told her. "The cows seemed fine when I milked this morning, but they've been dropping like flies ever since."

"Surely it's not the heat," she exclaimed, turning to Sam Gully, the veterinarian.

He was shaking his head. "I've never seen anything quite like it, but I'd say they've been poisoned somehow."

"Poisoned?" Liana replied in shock. "Do you think it was something in their feed?"

"Sam's having tests run on their grain, the grass, and the water," Dave explained. "Whatever it is, they've all gotten into it."

"Will they survive?" Nate wanted to know. He bent to examine the closest cow.

The farmers and the vet shook their heads. "They must have ingested a lot of poison," said Dave.

"Isn't there anything you can do?" Liana asked in amazement.

"The only thing we can do right now is to make sure they don't get any more poison and that it isn't spread to other livestock. Sam hopes to have some answers soon."

"You don't think it's a serious disease, do you?"

Nate asked, rising and slipping a supportive arm around Liana. She had gone from flushed to pale.

"I've never seen anything like it," said the vet. The farmers concurred. "We don't know if it's contagious or not. You fellows better get home and check your herds. If you notice anything out of the ordinary, call me."

Liana absently nodded a good-bye as the neighbors left. "You'll have to quarantine?"

"Until we know what kind of poison we're dealing with," said Dave.

Liana leaned against Nate for support. She let her eyes drift around the pasture at all the fallen livestock. It was a discouraging sight.

"Is there any way I can help?" Nate asked.

"We might need a backhoe if we have to bury any stock," said Dave, his tone grim.

Liana blinked back the tears that threatened. The dairy cattle were her dad's pride and joy. His dairy business was the economic mainstay of the farm. She didn't want to think about what such a loss might cost him. She had no knowledge of her parents' financial matters. Farming had fallen on some hard years. This could be devastating.

Nate suddenly went rigid, startling Liana. He said something terse that captured everyone's attention, and all eyes shifted toward the house. Smokey, the mischievous Pekingese, was trotting out to join them, but his short, fat body was staggering uncontrollably.

"Smokey!" Liana shouted in distress as she ran toward her sick pet. Nate followed closely and interceded when she would have scooped the Peke into her arms. He gently shoved her aside and lifted the dog off the ground. Liana crooned soothingly and stroked Smokey's head. Sam was beside them in an instant, examining the Peke.

"Sam, please, isn't there something you can do?" Liana asked hopefully.

"At least I can try with him," said the vet, taking Smokey from Nate and moving rapidly toward his van. "I can pump his stomach and try to lessen the effects. Then we'll have an actual sample of the poison."

"It has to be the water," declared Dave. "Smokey wouldn't have eaten anything the cows eat, but he drinks from the stream."

"You're probably right," agreed Sam. "That would explain why it's hitting the cows so hard and fast."

Dave, Liana, and Nate stayed near the barn while Sam took Smokey to his van for treatment. All they could do was stare at the dismal sight of fallen animals.

"Where does the stream originate?" Nate asked Dave.

"It's a natural southern flow from the artesian spring on your property," Dave told him. "In the sixty years I've lived here, I've never known it to be contaminated, even during the dog days of summer."

"I think I'll follow the stream back to the pond," Nate announced quietly. "I might find something; maybe a dead, infected animal or some evidence of deliberate contamination. I'll get the backhoe and be back shortly."

Dave nodded. "I'd appreciate that."

"Liana needs to get out of the sun and get some rest," Nate told the older man.

"I want to help," she argued in a weary tone. She knew she must look as exhausted as she felt.

"Why don't you help your mother in the kitchen. It's going to be a long day," Dave said.

Liana nodded in agreement, said good-bye to Nate, and headed for the house. She stopped by Sam's van to see what progress he was making, but he told her it would be a while before he knew whether Smokey would survive the poisoning.

Gloria was in the kitchen, and Liana gave her a fierce hug. "You must be worried sick."

"I am, honey, but it seems to be out of our hands."

"I'll help you cook. You'll probably be feeding hungry men the rest of the day."

Gloria scoured her face with worried eyes. "Why don't you take a shower and have a little nap. Then you'll be more help."

Liana knew she was right. She couldn't function when she was so exhausted. "Don't let me sleep too long."

"I won't."

The shower was brief. Liana wrapped her wet head in a towel and pulled on her terry robe. She returned to her room and sat down on the bed. She didn't really want to take a nap, but as soon as her head hit the pillow, she was asleep.

EIGHT

It was dinnertime when Nate entered the Banner home later that same evening. Gloria sent him to the upstairs bathroom to wash his hands and face. He agreed to wake Liana.

It wasn't hard to locate her room, and the door was ajar, so Nate stepped inside. He stopped dead still at the sight of her lovely body spread in sensual abandon on the bed. A violent shudder quaked over his body.

The towel had slipped off her head, and her hair tumbled around her head and shoulders like a fluffy blond cloud. The sides of her robe had parted to expose a wide stretch of creamy flesh down the center of her body. The soft curves of her breasts kept the fabric anchored, but the teasing glimpse of flesh was more erotic than nudity.

Nate's lungs constricted painfully. His reaction to Liana was raw and primitive. He wanted her badly, but not just physically. He felt a violent mixture of tenderness, possessiveness, and raging desire. His hunger for her was an emotional and physical challenge beyond his experience.

Stepping closer to the bed, he reached slightly unsteady hands to carefully draw the sides of her robe together. She'd be embarrassed to know he'd seen her in such a vulnerable state. He didn't want her to be defensive or uncomfortable with him.

Nate realized, with shocking insight, that he wanted Liana to trust him; unconditionally. He wanted it more than he'd ever wanted anything in his life, and that bothered him. They had little or nothing in common, he argued mentally. Their backgrounds were grossly different. There could be no future in a relationship between them.

He sat on the edge of the bed and reached a hand out to gently cup her cheek. She was so soft. His hands were rough, but he couldn't resist the urge to stroke her smooth skin. He spoke softly to her, and watched her lashes sweep upward to reveal sleep-clouded blue eyes.

"Nate?" Liana thought she must be dreaming. Nate Harden shouldn't be in her bed. She strained to focus her sleepy eyes on the man beside her. His touch was warm and gentle as he caressed her cheek and neck.

His oh-so-gorgeous eyes were regarding her with unblinking intensity. Liana couldn't remember any man ever looking at her with so much undisguised longing. Liquid heat flowed through her body. Nate's expression was mesmerizing, with an exciting combination of tenderness and desire.

"Time to wake up, sleepyhead." He sunk his fingers into the thickness of her hair and gently combed them through the silky tangles.

Liana watched his lips moving, then watched his eyes as they shifted to her hair. Her breathing was shallow. He was so big and gentle and close. She found she liked having him close. She liked the smell and feel of him. She liked having him touch her. She was afraid to do anything that might break the intimate spell.

Nate knew he should head back downstairs. Instead, he lifted both hands to cradle Liana's face. The look in her eyes made his blood race.

"The prince is supposed to kiss the sleeping lady," whispered Liana.

"I'm no prince," Nate insisted gruffly, but his head was already dipping. He brushed his lips back and forth over hers until she moaned for more.

Liana slid her arms around his midriff and drew him against her body. Her nipples hardened the instant they felt the crush of his hard chest. Her hold on him tightened, and she flicked her tongue over the fullness of his mouth. They both emitted small, hungry moans, and then deepened the kiss until they were forced to drag in air.

They were staring at each other in dazed fascination when Gloria's voice called up to them. "Nate! Liana! It's almost time to eat!"

"I'm supposed to be waking you," Nate explained, forcing himself to withdraw from their embrace. He rose from the bed and headed for the door. "I'll tell your mom that you'll be down in a few minutes."

The door closed quietly behind him, and Liana dragged in a ragged breath. Wow! Nate Harden had a powerful effect on her. He was an enigma, but she was totally captivated by his capacity for tenderness and passion.

Liana dressed quickly. By the time she made it to the kitchen, Gloria already had the food on the table.

"I was a lot of help, wasn't I?" Her tone was derisive as she gave her mother a hug.

"You needed the rest or you wouldn't have slept so long," put in Dave as he, Sam, and Nate entered the kitchen from the living room.

"I suppose," said Liana. "but I probably won't sleep a wink tonight."

"Let's eat while the food's hot," Gloria suggested as everyone took a place at the table.

Dave said grace, and they ate in relative silence. They'd finished dessert and were sipping coffee before Liana brought up the subject utmost in their minds.

"Are the cows going to live?"

"Yes, thankfully," said Dave. "They'll be weak and we'll lose the milk for a while, but we aren't going to lose the herd." His relief was evident.

"What did you find?" she asked the vet.

"The poison was a common insecticide. Once we had it identified, we were able to administer an antidote. There shouldn't be any side effects or long-term problems."

"Thank God," Liana said. "Smokey?"

"You know that dog's too ornery to die," her dad said. "He's asleep on the porch."

Liana grinned. She shifted her eyes to Nate, but was surprised at the tight expression on his face.

"What's worrying you?" she asked him, without considering how personal her question might sound.

"What's worrying me is how the poison got into the water supply in the first place."

"It wasn't an accidental runoff from a nearby field?"

"No," Nate responded in a heavy tone. "I followed the stream back to the pond and found empty insecticide containers. Somebody deliberately dumped it into the pond."

Liana's eyes widened in surprise. "Are you sure someone wasn't just careless with their trash?"

All three men were shaking their heads negatively. Nate answered her question. "The chemical company is applying insecticide in several fields in the area, but none are within a mile of the pond. Somebody had to take the chemicals to the pond and dump them, knowing the effect it would have on the herd's drinking supply."

"Whoever did it," added Sam, "knew approximately how much of the stuff would poison the cows without killing them. If one more container had been used, or the poison had been less diluted, the whole herd would have been killed."

"Someone deliberately poisoned your cows?" Liana exclaimed in disbelief. "Who would do such an evil thing, and why?" A glance passed between Dave and Nate that made Liana add, "You must have a suspicion. What's going on?"

Dave let Nate explain. "We don't think anyone was trying to kill the herd, but somebody definitely wants to cause trouble. They left the evidence on my property."

"Why?"

"To make it look like Nate was responsible for negligence, at best," Dave explained.

"My guess is that somebody doesn't want me settling in the area," Nate remarked grimly.

"So they maliciously poisoned our water supply?"

"That's the only logical reason we've come up with," Sam told her. "Your dad's too well known and liked by his neighbors. Nate's new in the area, so he's more than likely the target."

"But why? Why should anyone want to cause you trouble?" Liana asked Nate. She belatedly remembered that his mother had been forced to leave Springdale. "You don't think that anyone is holding a grudge against you and your mother, do you?"

Liana was aware that her parents exchanged relieved glances. They'd obviously been concerned about her reaction to the circumstances of Nate's illegitimacy.

"Mom learned that my biological father was killed in Vietnam," Nate explained without embarrassment. "He has three younger brothers living in Springdale, but your mom and dad don't think they're responsible."

Liana badly wanted to know who the three men were, but she didn't want to ask. Had Nate met them? Had he discussed the details of his parentage with anyone besides her parents? Sam seemed to know. Was she the only one who hadn't known?

It was hard to imagine who might have a grudge against Nate. Everyone she'd talked to seemed pleased that the Drenasis farm was being developed again, and the whole community had warmly welcomed Nate.

"Well, we'd better get back to work," said Dave as he finished his coffee. The men agreed and rose from the table.

"Can I help?" asked Liana.

"No, thanks, honey," Dave insisted. "There's not much more to do now. We just have to clean the barn, settle the herd for the night, and gather Sam's equipment. We'll be done in an hour or so."

"Okay," said Liana. Her eyes went to Nate. She didn't want him to leave. She had to be satisfied with the small smile he managed for her.

Gloria began to clear the table, and Liana took the dirty plates from her hands. "The least I can do is clean the kitchen," she insisted. "You have to be exhausted. Why don't you relax for a little while."

Her mother didn't argue, but she didn't relax, either. "If you really don't mind doing the dishes, I think I'll go out to the barn with your dad for a while."

"That's fine. I'll clean in here."

Gloria took off her apron, folded it, and laid it over a chair. She started out the back door, but Liana halted her progress.

"Nate told me about his mother and grandfather, but he didn't tell me who his father is . . . was," Liana corrected. "Did you know him well?"

Gloria's smile was sad. "He was a good man who had most of the responsibility for raising his brothers. That's how Mr. Drenasis convinced Olive to marry someone else. He threatened to destroy Jay's family if she didn't cooperate. He was very powerful and wealthy at that time, so she didn't doubt that he would carry out his threats."

"Jay?"

"Jay Newsome," Gloria told her.

Liana's eyes widened. Everyone in Springdale knew the Newsome family. They owned a very successful family farm-cooperative that involved hundreds of acres in the area. She'd heard stories about their brother who'd been killed in Vietnam. His name was engraved on a memorial at the town park.

"Why wouldn't Mr. Drenasis have approved of Jay Newsome for his daughter's husband?"

"At the time, Jay's family was just getting started in farming. They were poor, deeply in debt, and didn't have much social standing. Jay's hard work and determination had begun to pay off before he left for Vietnam, but not enough to impress Mr. Drenasis."

Liana shook her head and collected more dishes from the table. "I just can't imagine him being so cruel and heartless," she said, speaking of the elderly man she'd befriended. "He was always kind to me."

"By the time you started visiting him, I think he was regretting his treatment of Olive," explained Gloria. "The only reason your dad and I let you go over there is because we believed he desperately missed his daughter."

"Then why didn't he try to make amends? Do you think he tried to contact Nate's mother? Why didn't he leave his farm to his only child and grandchild?"

"I don't know," said Gloria. "Pride might have been the reason, or maybe he'd burned his bridges. I guess we'll never know."

"It's just such a shame," Liana insisted.

"It's sad," agreed Gloria. "But Olive and Nate have found their way back home. That's what's important."

"I guess you're right. We can't change the past,

but we can hope the future holds happiness for them.''

''We certainly can,'' declared Gloria as she turned to leave the house. ''I'm going out. Yell if you need me.''

Liana nodded and began to run water in the sink for the dishes. Her hands were busy for the next hour or so, but her thoughts were devoted to Nate. She couldn't get the man out of her mind.

Who would want to cause him trouble, and why? Who could be holding a grudge against a relative stranger? Was it someone who resented his arrival, or someone who wanted to make him pay for his grandfather's injustice?

Who would benefit if Nate and his mother were ostracized? Did someone want to discourage them from staying? Had Nate alienated someone from Springdale? A woman? Somebody's jealous husband?

Liana frowned. She didn't even know if Nate had dated anyone locally. She'd have to ask Jamie. He didn't fit her image of a playboy or a home wrecker. On the other hand, those eyes of his could wreak havoc on the female population with little effort.

Nate Harden was having a devastating effect on her, Liana admitted silently. New York had been full of handsome, charming men, but she hadn't met anyone who interested her beyond a casual date. None had made enough of an impact to replace Rod in her heart.

What she felt for Nate was totally unexpected, inexplicable, and a little scary. He excited her in the most elemental fashion. He challenged her on a very feminine level. Everything about him intrigued and fascinated her.

She was beginning to care too much for a man who undoubtedly had more experience with the opposite sex than she did. Despite the fact that he could be tender and thoughtful, his interest in her seemed purely physical.

Could she cope with that kind of a relationship? Liana knew she'd have to make a decision soon. Could she resist temptation? Did she want to?

It was after midnight before Liana went back upstairs. She wasn't the least bit sleepy, but she decided to take a cool bath and read awhile so that she wouldn't disturb her parents. They'd gone to bed early.

Nate had left without saying good night to her. That hurt. She knew she didn't have any right to complain, but she'd badly wanted to talk to him.

After a leisurely bath, Liana went to her room and turned on her radio. She stretched out on her bed and tried to concentrate on a romance novel. She was getting involved in the plot when she heard a noise at one of her windows.

Thinking it was just the wind or branches from a tree, she went back to her story. Then she heard the sound again. Something was being bounced off the window screen.

Liana tightened her robe and went to the window facing the barnyard. She lifted the screen and stuck her head out far enough to see the ground. The moon was full and bright enough to illuminate the whole area.

What she saw below her window made her heart skip a beat, then race madly. It was Nate, with one hand full of rocks, and his features carved in a warm, beckoning smile.

"Hi," he called to her softly, seductively.

No one word had ever had such a devastating impact on her senses. Liana felt a wild mixture of exhilaration, excitement, and anticipation.

"Hi, yourself." Her voice was equally warm and welcoming.

Nate's smile widened. "Want to come out and play?"

Liana's pulse raced. He was irresistible. She found his eyes and husky tone totally beguiling. There was no way she could have refused his invitation.

"It's awfully late," she argued, not wanting to appear too eager.

"I'm awfully lonesome." The sincerity of Nate's tone tugged at her heartstrings.

"I'm not dressed," she countered in a loud whisper. She didn't want her parents to hear their exchange.

Nate's voice was a little hoarse when he responded. "I'll wait."

"I won't be long," said Liana before ducking back into her room and quickly shedding her robe. She pulled on a pair of bikini underwear, blue jogging shorts, and a blue plaid cotton blouse. She didn't bother with a bra, but knotted the tails of her blouse beneath her breasts.

Her hair was clipped on top of her head with a wide barrette. Liana unclasped the barrette and quickly brushed out all the tangles, leaving her hair draped over her shoulders. Then she slipped on canvas shoes and headed back to the window.

"I'm coming down," she called before thrusting a leg through the window. She found a firm foothold on the old trellis and eased herself down the side of the house. Nate's hands were waiting to help her to the ground.

At the first touch of his rough palms against her bare calves, Liana felt a jolt of hot reaction. Her legs quivered, but Nate's big hands lent her the strength to reach the ground safely.

His hands slid to her waist, and he turned her in his arms. They grinned at each other like naughty, but supremely self-satisfied, children. "This is a pretty awesome escape route," Nate told her. "I always had to climb out on a roof and shinny down a tree."

"My sisters and I used this on a fairly regular basis," Liana explained. "Daddy says he keeps the trellis in good repair for emergencies."

"And you've never been caught coming or going?"

"We used to think we were fooling Mother and Daddy. Then Beth got involved with some guy they didn't trust. Mother grew roses on the trellis that summer."

"Ouch! Thorns, huh?" Nate said with a laugh. He put some distance between them. "Tell me about your sisters," he urged as he turned toward the barnyard.

"Where are we going?" Liana asked, grasping hold of his arm. "How did you get here?"

Nate took hold of her hand. It felt good to entwine their fingers. "I walked. I wanted to check the pond again tonight. Everything's fine, but I didn't feel like going back to the house. You said you probably wouldn't be able to sleep, so I thought we could keep each other company."

"I'm glad you thought that," she declared lightly,

giving his hand a squeeze. They began to walk through the soft grass of the yard.

"So? Are you going to tell me about your sisters?"

"Beth is the oldest, and despite her poor taste in men, she managed to latch on to a really great guy. They're married and live in Cleveland."

The ground got rougher as they reached the barnyard. Liana continued. "She made a quick visit when I first came home, but I wasn't very good company. It seems like ages since we really spent time together."

"And Emily?"

Liana laughed softly. "You know all about my sisters and me already," she charged. "I'm sure Mother and Daddy have told you more stories than you ever wanted to hear."

"You haven't told me."

Her smile stayed firmly in place as she described her other sister. "Emily's a registered nurse, as you probably know. She lives and works in Columbus with her husband, who's also in the medical profession."

They paused a minute to look at the dairy cattle. Dave had penned them in a fenced area near the barn. The cows were all looking much stronger and healthier.

"I'm glad they'll be okay," said Liana.

"So am I," added Nate as they began walking again. "I'm just sorry it had to happen in the first place."

"I know, but there's nothing you could have done," she insisted. She knew he was blaming himself for the poisoning, but it wasn't his fault. "Nobody could have anticipated such a cruel trick."

Nate didn't respond. Liana knew he was angry that someone would deliberately harm others to get at him.

They walked awhile in silence. When they entered the woods, they lost the light of the moon and had to be more careful. He pulled Liana closer to his side, and in a few minutes they were at the fence of his property.

Nate determinedly put thoughts of the poisoning out of his mind. He didn't want anything interfering with the time he and Liana shared. "So tell me about your sisters," he repeated as they climbed the fence.

Liana rolled her eyes. "I just told you about them."

"You told me what I already know," he argued. "I want to know about your relationship with them."

"Okay," she agreed on a sigh, "but first you have to assure me that there's no poison ivy out here."

"The whole area was sprayed."

"Glad to hear it."

"Are you all healed?"

"Totally," Liana told him. "How about you?"

"I'm fine. I didn't have it that bad."

Liana squeezed his hand. They'd reached the circle of boulders beside the pond. She slid to the ground and tugged Nate down beside her. They used a flat-sided boulder as a backrest, and stretched their legs in front of them.

"I guess my sisters and I had a fairly normal relationship," Liana finally explained. She took Nate's hand in both of hers and absently caressed his strong fingers.

"We were always either giggling or fighting. There never seemed to be a happy medium. We argued over clothes, boys, and whose turn it was to do the dishes. Just the regular stuff. If we were happy and in good moods, everything was funny."

"Sounds nice," Nate commented as he shifted closer to her. He buried one hand in her hair and let the silky tresses spill through his fingers.

"Nice, normal, average, boring," Liana retorted. "I can't remember ever doing anything wild and uninhibited. I am a slave to convention." She loved the feel of his fingers in her hair.

Nate had never done anything conventional in his life. Making the move to Springdale was the closest he'd ever come. Nice, normal, and average had great appeal to him.

That was part of the reason he was so fascinated by Liana. He knew their backgrounds were too different to ever allow them a future. He would always be the bad boy, and she would always be the small-town princess.

"The moon is really bright tonight," Liana remarked when Nate was quiet for too long. "It's almost comfortable here by the water." The temperature was still high, but the night had brought a drop in humidity.

"This is my favorite part of the farm," said Nate as he looked at the pond with its halo of weeping willow trees.

"It's always been my favorite, too," Liana told him. "Mr. Drenasis let my friends and me swim here in the summer."

"Tell me about it," Nate urged while pulling her closer. He sat her between his legs, and wrapped his arms around her waist, locking his hands beneath her breasts. Then he rested his face in her sweet-smelling hair.

Liana liked being cradled by his hard, warm body. She felt vibrantly alive and totally feminine in his arms. Resting her back against his chest and her head against his shoulder, she gave him more details about her youth.

"When we were in high school, my sisters and I always held Fourth of July celebrations here at the pond so that we could swim. In the fall we had wiener roasts with a big bonfire here at the boulders. If the temperatures got cold enough, we could even ice-skate on one section of the pond."

"Sounds like fun," Nate murmured, even though he'd never had much experience with fun.

"Tell me about your childhood," Liana encouraged gently. "You said your stepfather was a crony of Mr. Drenasis. Was he a lot older than your mother?"

"He was twenty-five years older than she."

"Was he a good man?"

Nate hesitated a long time before answering. Liana felt the sudden tension in his body. She almost regretted her question, but couldn't deny her interest in his past.

"Buford Harden was a good farmer, and he taught me to love and respect the land," Nate finally replied.

His hold on Liana had tightened. She didn't think he realized how strong his grip was. She had a feeling he never talked about his childhood, and that it was difficult for him. She held her breath in hopes that he would share more of himself with her.

When he was quiet too long, her next question was asked in a very tentative tone. "Did you love him?"

There was nothing tentative about Nate's response. "I hated him."

NINE

Thousands of stars twinkled in the sky above them. They were being treated to a chorus of summertime sounds: croaking toads, chirping crickets, the hooting of an owl. The breeze was soft and scented with wild honeysuckle. Liana was cocooned in the arms of a strong, tender man.

All her life had been the same. She'd been raised with love and laughter. Her emotional security had been one of her parents' highest priorities. She'd been protected, respected, and cherished.

The word "hate" had never been a part of Liana's vocabulary. Her mother wouldn't allow it. There were plenty of things that she didn't like, but she'd never hated anything or anyone. She didn't even know how. Nate's tone implied that he knew too much about hate.

"Can you talk about it?" she asked him while she stroked the arms that enfolded her.

He never had, but Liana was easy to talk to.

"When I was little, I thought it was normal for a dad to be cold and hard. My mom provided the love and caring. As I grew older, I realized she had to fight him for every small favor or treat she wanted for me," he explained.

"I worked hard and tried to please him, but he wanted a son of his own. He blamed Mom for not conceiving. He started drinking heavily, and I started to hear more of the mental abuse he'd used on her for years. When I was thirteen, he told me I wasn't his son, that I was a bastard. He never let another day go by without reminding me."

A strangled sound escaped Liana's throat, and she pressed herself closer to Nate, offering what little comfort she could. She couldn't bear to think about the emotional pain, confusion, and rejection he must have endured.

"You were a teenager before you realized he wasn't your natural father?"

"Uh-huh," said Nate. He closed his eyes and shuddered at the memories of humiliation and rejection. He'd never told another living soul about those dark years.

"You must have been so hurt and confused."

"It hurt at first, but the older I got, the happier I was that we had no biological link between us."

Nate dropped his mouth to the curve of Liana's neck and kissed her with warm, hungry lips. He didn't want to think about the past, just the woman in his arms. He ached for her. He was nearly mindless with wanting.

Despite the blaring differences in their backgrounds, the attraction between them couldn't be denied. Nate knew he was probably a fool for succumbing to temptation, but his desire was stronger than his common sense.

Liana arched her neck. She loved the feel of his mouth on her skin. She felt his thighs tightening around her hips, and squirmed against him.

Nate brought his hands up to cup the fullness of her unbound breasts. Her nipples immediately hardened against his palms, and his breath shattered. The evidence of her arousal created a deep, throbbing need in his body.

Liana felt Nate's body growing hard with arousal. His mouth was hot on her neck and was sending shivers over her body. His hands molded and adored her breasts. His thumbs teased each nipple until she grew too restless to sit still. She shifted in his arms until she was lying flat on her back in the soft grass.

Nate leaned over her and captured her lips with his mouth. He curved one arm above her head and wound his fingers through her hair. His other hand continued to caress her breasts until Liana was moaning into his mouth.

He thrust his tongue through her lips and challenged hers to a sparring match. Liana's mouth was hot and hungry and sweet. When she sucked his tongue deeply into her mouth, fire rocketed through him, and he struggled to contain his impatience.

He dragged his mouth from hers, and their breath poured out in a mingled groan. Their eyes locked and smoldered with a need too intense to deny.

"You told me you and Rod had never been lovers," Nate rasped, his eyes dark and searching. His hand cupped her cheek, and his thumb brushed over her moist lips.

"Did you just say that to make me mad or is it the truth?" he demanded thickly.

Liana's chest was heaving and her breathing was rough. She knew what he was asking, and she answered as succinctly as possible. "Rod and I never had sexual intercourse."

A tortured groan rumbled from Nate's chest. If Liana hadn't had sex with Rod, he knew she hadn't had it with anyone else. He started to withdraw from their embrace.

Liana wrapped her arms around his waist and pulled him closer. She didn't want him to think she was totally inexperienced. He wanted to know if she was a virgin. She wanted to explain without going into too much detail about her relationship with Rod.

"Rod is the only other man I ever wanted," she explained in a husky tone. "He decided we wouldn't have sex until we married. I spent lots of time trying to change his mind, and he concentrated on teaching me other ways of loving."

Nate's muscles coiled into knots. Rod had known how to love Liana. He wasn't sure he did. He wrapped his arms around her and cushioned his head on her breasts. His next words were full of self-derision.

"You've never had sex, just love. I've never had love, just sex."

His admission tore at Liana's heart. She desperately wanted him to accept her loving. "We could teach each other," she whispered.

Nate's breath poured out in an agonized groan. He nuzzled his face against Liana's breasts and then slowly kissed his way up her slender throat to her lips. He captured her mouth with renewed urgency.

Their tongues met; hot and wet and seeking. They kissed for long, breathless minutes, dragged some air into their lungs, and kissed again. Nate eased his body more fully over Liana's, intimately rubbing his hard angles against her soft curves.

"I don't want to hurt you," he murmured thickly against her lips.

"You won't, I promise." Her body was screaming for his touch. His reluctance was the only thing hurting her.

"Tell me what you want," Nate coaxed gruffly.

Liana nudged his head down to her breasts again. His hands shook as he untied the knot of her blouse. With each button he released, he gave her a warm, moist kiss on the tender skin he bared.

When her blouse was completely unfastened, he shoved the sides apart and gazed at the loveliness of her breasts. With a hoarse moan, he dipped his head and took one taut nipple in his mouth while his fingers sought the other.

He kissed, licked, and suckled each nipple with a single-minded concentration that soon had Liana moaning and writhing beneath him. Her fingers clutched in his hair as he continued to lavish attention on her breasts.

"Nate!" she whispered in a tortured breath.

"You're beautiful," he ground out roughly. He lifted his head long enough to share another feverish kiss, and then his hands and eyes roved farther down her body.

"I want to see all of you." Nate's eyes sought permission while his fingers tugged at the waist of her shorts. Liana lifted her hips in answer to his unspoken question.

When she was totally exposed to the night air and his brilliant gaze, a tremor coursed over her. She felt more vulnerable than she'd ever felt in her life, and far more aroused than she'd imagined possible.

Nate laid a hand on her thigh and felt her soft, supple flesh. He could hear the blood pounding in his head. No woman had ever excited him as much as Liana. No woman had ever brought him so close to losing control. She hadn't even touched him, and he was ready to explode.

Liana tugged at his shirt and pulled it from the waistband of his jeans. Nate helped her drag it over his head and toss it aside. They moaned in unison when the tight curls of his chest tangled with her taut nipples.

"Kiss me!" he begged hoarsely.

The kiss was hotter and more feverish than all the others. Their arms and legs entwined while their tongues dueled passionately. Nate thrust his tongue in and out of her mouth as a prelude to the same mating of their bodies.

Liana slid a hand between them and searched for the snap of his jeans. She wanted him naked, too, but she got distracted by the hard bulge beneath the denim. She stroked him until he began to buck against her body.

The hot, aching heaviness in his groin intensified until Nate thought he would shatter in a million pieces. He withstood a few glorious, torturous minutes of her caresses, then shifted out of her reach to strip off the rest of his clothes. He grabbed a packet of protection from his jeans and kicked them off his legs.

When Liana reached for him again, he twisted

away from her roaming fingers. "Don't touch me," he rasped. His breathing was hot and labored. "Please! I can't stand any more!" His control was nearly nonexistent.

Liana kept her hands above his waist, but her fingers soon found the taut nipples buried in the golden curls on his chest. She smiled with sensual satisfaction when he uttered a low, agonized moan. She used her tongue to draw forth more erotic sounds of excitement.

It was Nate's turn to smile when his fingers slipped up her leg to the juncture of her thighs. Liana gasped at his touch, then moaned in pleasure as he gently stroked her most sensitive flesh.

"You're so hot and soft," he praised in a thick tone. "I want to feel all of you, but not until you're ready."

His fingers explored more sensitive flesh. Liana whimpered and arched her hips against his hand. The sounds, smell, and feel of her arousal sent a violent tremor quaking over Nate's body. The only way he could contain his own raging desire was to concentrate on the woman in his arms.

His mouth found one of her turgid nipples, and this time he sucked roughly, greedily. Liana stifled a scream as the tension in her body mounted to staggering heights. Her nails dug into his shoulders as Nate's caresses drove her to a fever pitch of need.

"Please, Nate! Please! Please!" she begged as her body writhed beneath his.

"Do you want me?" he grated as his lips left her breast and hovered over her mouth.

Liana dragged his head closer and clutched at his hair while she seared his lips with her own. Nate wrapped his arms around her and lifted her gently while positioning himself between her thighs.

A moan got trapped in her throat as she felt Nate's hard, smooth flesh penetrating her body. Nothing in her experience had prepared her for such intimacy. She tensed, but his skillful caresses and softly crooning voice quickly helped her relax. Then, with only a brief flash of pain, Liana felt his body locked with hers.

Nate's body was soaked in sweat. He was fighting a feverish desire for completion. He forced himself to remain perfectly still until Liana could adjust to the feel of him. He would not hurt her.

They clung to each other, their bodies trembling with tension, their eyes locked.

"Is this how you make love?" Nate found the strength to ask.

Liana's breath caught on a sob. "Yes, yes!" she exclaimed as renewed tension coiled within her body. "Is this good sex?"

"The best!" growled Nate as she started to rock her hips against him in demand. "The very best."

Neither of them had enough energy to speak as their bodies began to dance in the age-old rhythm of love. The sounds they made were private, primitive, and pleasing.

Liana sobbed as her body found a release from the incredible tension. Nate watched her with gleaming eyes and held her tightly until the first wave of pleasure passed.

Then they soared again. The pleasure was unbearable. Nate felt waves of release rippling along his spine, and it washed over him like a tidal wave. This time they reached the stars together.

He collapsed in her arms, and they both fought for breath. When he had the strength, he rolled onto his back and pulled Liana on top of him. His arms encircled her and held her possessively.

Nate had never known such overwhelming satisfaction. It wasn't just the great sex, or the lesson in loving, but the woman in his arms. Liana made everything special. She was sunshine, sweetness, and spice. She made him feel whole.

She scared the hell out of him. He wanted too much from her. He knew it was a mistake to want anything or anyone as much as he wanted Liana. Fate had never been kind to him, so he didn't expect favors, and he was instinctively wary of happiness.

His life had been one long, continuous battle. He'd fought for everything he ever had, and had broken plenty of rules along the way. He was finally trying to live the life he really wanted, but he couldn't erase the past, and he was never going to be the Prince Charming she deserved.

Liana's head was resting on Nate's shoulder. When her breathing returned to normal, she placed a soft kiss on his neck. His skin tasted salty. She kissed him again.

"I thought you might have fallen asleep on me." Nate's tone was light even though her kisses were sending ripples of pleasure through him.

"I'm not the least bit sleepy," Liana muttered against his throat. Then she kissed his ear.

Nate began to caress her back with gentle hands. She felt good in his arms and against his body; like a necessary extension of himself. He didn't want to think about having to let her go.

Liana put her hands in the grass on either side of

his head. She lifted herself high enough to look him in the eyes. Her smile was adoring.

Nate wanted to say something profound. He wanted to describe the turbulent emotions churning in him, but he couldn't find the words. He wasn't sure he could even define his feelings. The tenderness, possessiveness, and fascination were all too new to him.

Liana's hair was cloaking them in a web of intimacy. The warmth of her smile made his heart throb painfully. Nate finally managed to speak.

"Thank you," he whispered huskily.

Liana's smile widened, and her eyes sparkled with tears. She brushed her nose back and forth across his and then dropped a kiss on his lips. He was the one who deserved the thanks, but her throat was too tight to allow the words.

"I didn't hurt you?"

Liana shook her head.

"You're not going to regret this, are you?"

"No!" Liana insisted fiercely. She was very much in love with him, but she wasn't ready to confess her secret. She didn't even know when or how it had happened, only that she was hopelessly in love.

"You're not going to regret this, are you?" She tossed his question back at him.

Nate's arms tightened around her. "How could I regret making love to you?"

Liana's pulse accelerated. "It wasn't just great sex?" She wanted to believe their loving had meant as much to him as it had to her.

Nate rolled her to her back and pressed her against the warm earth with his warm body. "It was great sex," he swore gruffly, "but a whole lot more."

Liana sighed her satisfaction and lifted her head to

press a kiss on his lips. Her arms circled his waist as they shared a long, sweet kiss. Her grip tightened as the desire between them began to escalate.

Nate felt all the blood rushing to his groin again. His need for Liana was insatiable. He'd thought that loving her would satisfy the need, but it only intensified it. He wanted so much more than he had the right to ask for.

"Are we going to have another lesson?" she whispered into his mouth. She felt him growing hard against her thighs, and was instantly aroused by the knowledge that he wanted her again.

Nate's groan trembled between their lips. "We can't," he insisted thickly. "I can't protect you."

It was Liana's turn to groan. "Couldn't we take a tiny little chance?"

"No." Nate was adamant. He rose from the ground and pulled Liana to her feet. His eyes locked with hers while he explained. "My parents took chances, and I'm a bastard. I'll never risk fathering an unwanted child."

Liana respected his decision. "I'll try not to tempt you," she promised.

Nate's smile was stiff. She was a walking, breathing temptation. Until Liana, he'd never met a woman he couldn't walk away from, or one he couldn't resist. She was different.

"I think we need a bath," he suggested gruffly. He was hoping to cool his desire.

Liana was still wearing her blouse. She slipped her arms out of the sleeves and let it fall to the ground. Nate picked her up, and her arms slid around his neck.

"Is the pond safe?"

"Sam tested it earlier," Nate told her as he walked toward the water. "He said it's fine."

Liana gasped at the initial chill of the water against her overheated flesh. Then she sighed with pleasure at the erotic feel of the water on her naked body. Nate let her feet slide to the bottom of the pool, but kept a firm grip on her slippery body.

"I don't want you to do anything energetic," he said. "Just relax and enjoy the water."

Their slick bodies rubbed against each other and created a new ache of arousal. Liana fought the urge to grind her hips against his.

"I think I'd better do a few laps," Nate ground out tersely. It was agony to let her go, but the thought of making love in the water was far too exciting.

Liana stayed close to the bank and watched as Nate's hard, athletic body cut wide arcs through the water. He was tanned and strong and gorgeous. She knew she'd never tire of looking at him.

Nate's powerful body was creating waves that washed rhythmically over Liana's body and kept her nerve endings highly sensitized. Desire rippled through her with each wave. If she was going to help him resist temptation, she needed to get out of the pond and get dressed.

As she climbed from the water, Nate slowed his frantic pace and watched her. Her graceful, shapely body glistened in the moonlight. His chest constricted at the sight of her pagan beauty.

For the first time in his life, he didn't want to be parted from a woman for even a little while. He wanted Liana close to him, by his side, in his arms.

He'd never felt that way about any woman, and he wasn't coping very well with the new emotions.

Liana squeezed the excess water from her hair. The ends were the only soaked part, and she knew they'd dry quickly. Her body was still damp as she pulled on her clothing, but she couldn't stay nude for long. Despite her shared intimacy with Nate, she wasn't used to having anyone see her naked.

Nate wasn't so modest. He pulled himself from the pond and shook off the excess water with little thought of his nudity. Liana's pulse beat loudly in her ears at the unrestricted sight of his sheer male beauty. She wanted to reach out and touch him, but knew she couldn't do it.

"What big eyes you have, nymph," Nate teased. Her eyes on him made him hot. The cool water and exercise had done little to dampen his desire.

Liana was totally enthralled by his body's reaction to her perusal. She studied him awhile longer, then gave him a saucy grin and covered her eyes with her hands.

"Better late than never," Nate taunted. He moved within inches of her and gave her a swift, hard kiss, making sure their bodies didn't touch at any point but their mouths. Then he reached for his own clothes and dressed.

"Can I uncover my eyes now?" she asked at the sound of his jeans being zipped.

Nate slipped on his shirt and drew Liana into his arms. "I never told you to cover them in the first place," he said.

Liana's arms slid over his chest to lock around his neck. "You were teasing me about my innate curiosity," she challenged.

"I think you've satisfied your curiosity about a lot of things tonight."

She grinned, and her eyes sparkled with mischief. "I've only begun to satisfy my curiosity about you."

Nate brushed his lips lightly across hers. "I don't know if I can stand much more temptation, but I don't want the night to end."

"Me either," Liana whispered. "I wish we could run away from home."

"Where would you like to go?"

Liana kissed him lightly. "A secluded beach house. An isolated mountain cabin. A hidden cottage in a woods far from home," she told him.

Nate moaned and hugged her closer. He'd like nothing more than to have Liana all to himself for days, maybe weeks. Just the thought made him delirious.

"Too bad we're such slaves to convention," she added with a touch of disgust.

"Too bad," Nate reiterated with feeling. The conventional solution was marriage and a very long honeymoon. His thoughts were beginning to conform to convention. It was dangerous to even consider the possibility.

"I'd better walk you home," he said after stealing another kiss. "You've had a long day, and I don't want you to get sick again."

Liana agreed, and they started walking. They kept their arms around each other as they slowly made their way across the fields to the house.

When they reached the trellis under her bedroom window, Nate turned her more fully into his arms and kissed her until neither of them could breathe. Then she claimed another long, satisfying kiss.

When their mouths finally parted, Liana's lips trembled with the need to say, "I love you," but she didn't utter the words aloud. She wasn't sure how Nate would react. She didn't know how to react herself, and she definitely didn't want to alienate him.

"Thank you for tonight," he muttered against her lips as he stole one last kiss.

"Thank you for making it so special," she replied huskily. Then she carefully climbed the trellis to her room.

TEN

It seemed as if she'd just closed her eyes when the shrill ringing of the telephone broke into Liana's sleep. She tried to ignore the jarring sound, but then her mother's voice floated up the stairs.

"Liana, it's Jamie, and it's important!"

Her arms and legs didn't want to function properly. It was an effort to climb out of bed, wrap herself in a robe, and get down the stairs.

"Jamie?" Liana mumbled sleepily as she took the receiver from her mother.

"Liana, Rod's been in an accident."

Jamie's trembling tone and her frightening announcement shocked Liana wide-awake. "What happened? Where is he? How bad was it?"

"He's at the county hospital, and I'm here with him," Jamie explained with more control. "He was in a car wreck sometime last night. The sheriff couldn't reach his parents, so he called me."

"Is he all right?"

"He hit his head pretty hard," Jamie said, her voice choked again. "He's still unconscious."

Panic ripped through Liana. A serious head injury. She tried to remain calm. "Where are Rod's parents?"

"They went to Lake Erie for the weekend," Jamie explained. "I don't even know how to reach them."

"I'll be there as soon as I can get dressed."

"Thanks. Rod's in a private room. Number one-oh-three."

"I'll find you. Just try not to worry too much. He's strong. He'll be all right, I know it." Liana prayed even as she tried to reassure her friend.

"I'll see you in a little while," said Jamie.

Liana said good-bye and hung up the phone. "Rod has a head injury, and he's still unconscious," she told Gloria as she headed back up the stairs. "The Governs are at the lake. Do you have any idea how they can be reached?"

"They bought a cabin up there," said Gloria, "but there's no phone. I have the name of the nearest town in my address book. Maybe we can reach them through the sheriff's department."

It took Liana half an hour to get dressed and drive to the hospital. The one-story facility was familiar, and she easily found Rod's room. Jamie greeted her with a hug.

"Has there been any change?" Liana asked as she moved to the side of Rod's bed. He looked pale beneath the cuts and bruises on his face. She could see a huge lump on his forehead. She reached out to stroke his cheek gently.

"The doctors are monitoring brain waves, and everything seems normal. They said his skull wasn't fractured, but he has a severe concussion. They also said he'd regain consciousness soon, but he hasn't!''

''Is he hurt anywhere else?''

''No, he was protected by his seat belt, but he hit the tree hard enough that his head cracked the windshield.''

Liana's stomach rolled at the thought. ''I passed the tow truck when I came to town,'' she told her friend. ''Rod's car looks like it's been in a demolition derby.''

''I don't even want to see it.''

''Does anybody know what happened?''

''The sheriff thinks someone deliberately ran Rod off the road.'' Jamie almost choked on the words.

''What? Why? Who?'' Liana demanded.

''He said there's blue paint along the left side of Rod's car. It looks like someone slammed into him repeatedly. He must have swerved too far to the right and hit the tree.''

''Why would anyone want to hurt Rod?'' Liana asked in amazement. She touched his hand and spoke softly to him, but there was no response. Jamie was quiet for a short time, and Liana looked directly at her friend. They stared at each other across Rod's bed.

''What is it?'' Liana demanded, knowing Jamie wanted to say something, but was reluctant to upset her. ''Does the sheriff know who did this to Rod?''

''He thinks somebody got angry because Rod was visiting you last night.''

''Rod didn't come to my house last night. At least, not that I know of. What time was the accident?''

''They think it was between one and two in the morning, but Rod wasn't found until four. The sheriff thinks Nate might have gotten jealous, caused the wreck, and then left Rod out there.''

"Nate! That's insane!" Liana exclaimed in a loud whisper. "He was with me most of the night. He came to my house about one and stayed until four. He couldn't have been involved."

"Someone saw Nate's truck heading out of town about the same time Rod was supposed to have wrecked," Jamie explained in a rush. "The sheriff went out to Nate's and found his pickup truck hidden in the barn. It's all smashed up and has red paint on it."

Nate's pickup truck was blue. Rod's car was red. Liana was shaking her head before the last word was out of her friend's mouth.

"No! No! No! That's ridiculous. Nate has no reason to hurt Rod. Jamie, you do know that Rod and I broke up at the party two weeks ago, don't you? There were no hard feelings, and Nate has no reason to be jealous."

"Rod said you'd decided not to see each other." Jamie's blush was the only spot of color on her unnaturally pale features. "But I thought maybe he was missing you."

"Not that I know of," Liana said. "He's crazy about you, you know."

Jamie's eyes immediately filled with tears. "I'm crazy about him, too, but I want him to be sure. I don't want him on the rebound, or if he still has strong feelings for you."

Liana stroked Rod's arm, fighting back her own tears. "I'm always going to love him, Jamie, just the same way I love you. Until I met Nate, I didn't realize that what Rod and I share isn't enough."

Jamie's eyes widened in surprise. "You're in love with Nate?"

Liana had admitted her feelings to herself, but wasn't comfortable with the words yet. "I'm pretty crazy about him," she confessed huskily.

"Oh my God, Liana! You have to get over to the sheriff's office and tell them Nate was with you last night. I heard a deputy say they were going to pick Nate up and question him. They might even throw him in jail."

Liana's eyes widened in shock. "It's not even seven o'clock," she argued. "Surely they wouldn't drag him out of bed at this time of morning. Sheriff Thompson isn't a fanatic."

Jamie rolled her eyes. "He might not be, but some of those deputies are certifiable lunatics."

"Even if Nate's truck was involved, they don't have any real evidence that he was driving," Liana argued.

"That's enough to bring Nate in for questioning."

Liana studied Rod's still features. She was torn between loyalties. She didn't want to leave him, yet she didn't want Nate to be harassed or humiliated.

"Go," Jamie insisted. "I already promised I'd call the sheriff's office as soon as Rod regains consciousness."

"I'll just tell Sheriff Thompson that Nate was with me, and then I'll be right back," Liana told her friend. She leaned over and gave Rod a light kiss on the cheek.

"Hurry up and get better," she whispered to the unconscious man. Then she scolded. "You've already scared Jamie and me out of our minds." Rod had always loved to provoke emotional reactions from the two of them.

The drive from the hospital to the sheriff's office was only a few miles, and Liana was there within minutes. She gave her name to the dispatcher on duty and was sent directly to the sheriff's private office.

Sheriff John Thompson was a big man. He stood as Liana entered the room, waved her to a seat, and then sat back down behind his desk. Except for the gray in his hair and a few more wrinkles, Liana didn't think he'd changed much in twenty years.

"It's good to see you, Liana. You look good. I hope you're feeling better."

Liana wasn't surprised by his comments. Like most people in Springdale, he'd watched her grow up and knew her life history. "I'm much better, thank you," she replied.

"Have you been to the hospital?" asked the sheriff. At her nod, he continued. "How's Rod?"

"There's no change, but Jamie said the doctors think he'll regain consciousness soon. I came over here to tell you Nate Harden didn't have anything to do with the wreck."

The sheriff's expression was impossible to read. Liana couldn't tell what he was thinking.

"I've talked to Harden. He says he doesn't know how his truck got battered, and he doesn't have an alibi for the hours between one and four."

"No alibi?" Liana repeated in disbelief.

"He told me he was at home in bed," the sheriff continued, "but Ned Larkin tried to find him about two and said he wasn't home. We're running tests on his truck, but there's little doubt that it's the other vehicle involved."

"Everybody on the farm drives that truck!" Liana insisted. "Nate leaves the keys in the ignition."

"That may be, but he lied about where he was."

Liana was shaking her head in frustration. "He lied to protect me," she argued. "He's a little old-fashioned and probably didn't want to tell you, but I swear he was with me most of the night."

The sheriff's bushy brows rose, and Liana felt herself blushing. She silently cursed a town full of people who thought they had the right to censure her behavior.

"I called your house this morning, too," the sheriff added. "Your mother said she didn't see Rod or Nate after midnight."

"As far as I know, Rod wasn't at my house last night," Liana explained. She decided to be very specific. Sheriff Thompson was familiar with her dad's property and would know exactly what she was describing. She also knew he wouldn't repeat a word of what she said.

"Nate walked across the field and threw rocks at my window. I climbed down the trellis, and the two of us spent a few hours out at the pond."

Sheriff Thompson's frown deepened, and he leaned forward on his desk. "Liana, you realize we're talking about attempted murder here, don't you? You wouldn't make up a story just to protect this guy, would you?"

"I would not," she replied succinctly. "I'm willing to swear, under oath, that Nate spent the hours between one and four with me. It's the absolute truth. I don't know why he had to be so silly and protective in the first place. He should have just told you the truth."

"Maybe he's worried about your reputation."

"Then he's the only one," she countered irritably. "My reputation isn't in nearly as much jeopardy as his. I don't care if the whole world knows Nate and I spent the night together."

The sheriff studied her intently for several minutes. "I've never known you to lie, Liana," he commented quietly.

She looked him directly in the eyes. "I'm not lying now."

The sheriff punched a button on his intercom. "Have Rondel bring Harden to my office, please."

"Nate's here now? You have him in jail?" Liana exclaimed in distress. "Why?"

"We brought him in for questioning and then charged him with attempted murder," the sheriff explained. "We're holding him until his lawyer gets here."

All the color washed out of Liana's face, and she rose to her feet. "On what evidence?" she cried.

"He owns the truck that was involved."

"Damn flimsy evidence!" she spouted angrily. "What about motive?"

"He lied about his whereabouts," the sheriff reminded, "and crimes of passion aren't that uncommon."

Liana closed her eyes briefly, reopened them, and began to pace the room in frustration. "Rod and I broke up two weeks ago. Rod's in love with Jamie Smith, and Nate realized it before I did. He has absolutely no reason to be jealous of Rod."

"I wish I'd known that."

Liana wondered if she should take out a newspaper advertisement to update the town on her personal business. She turned as the office door opened, and

Nate was ushered in by Ben Rondel. She'd always thought the deputy was a little short on brains.

Nate was wearing jeans and a dark T-shirt. He looked as if he'd been rudely awakened, and his expression was grim. His features could have been carved from stone, and the instant he saw her, his eyes grew colder.

Liana was momentarily stunned by the sight of a Nate she didn't know. Gone was the warmth of bedroom eyes she loved and trusted. He didn't show her a trace of tenderness.

"You can take off the handcuffs, Rondel."

The sheriff's words sent shock waves through Liana. She belatedly realized that Nate's hands were behind his back, and that he was handcuffed. Her temper flared.

"Handcuffs!" she cried in agitation. "Have you all taken leave of your senses!" she nearly shouted at the officers. "You have no real evidence, no witnesses, and no motive, yet you've got Nate in chains!" she screeched, moving closer to him.

"I'm all right," Nate told her, but his tone didn't encourage her to get any closer.

"Calm down, Liana," the sheriff soothed. "Take the cuffs off, Rondel."

The deputy sputtered with indignation. "I'm not so sure that's a good idea, sheriff," he defended. "This man has a record. He's a convicted felon."

A dead silence fell over the room. Nate made a rough sound, and the sheriff made an even rougher one. Thompson didn't hide his displeasure at the deputy's disclosure of privileged information.

Liana's eyes sought Nate's. Instead of repelling her, the deputy's declaration urged her closer to him as if her presence could ward off the ugliness of the accusation.

The sheriff ordered his deputy from the room, and Rondel quickly left with the handcuffs.

Nate rubbed his wrists, but his eyes never left Liana. "I killed a man once," he stated baldly. The words were said with a total lack of expression. He appeared so devoid of emotion that Liana felt a chill run over her.

If she'd been meeting him for the first time, she might have mistaken his iron control for sheer arrogance. At the moment, he looked capable of taking a life without blinking an eye.

This wasn't the man she loved. This was a cold impostor he used to protect a much more sensitive man. Liana had a mental image of Nate gently scooping Smokey into his arms when he was sick. She remembered his eyes when he'd made love to her, and his pain when he'd talked about a childhood that had taught him how to hide within himself.

The cold arrogance was a method of self-defense. It hurt to think of how many times he must have been forced to mentally block out all emotion.

"Your stepfather?" she queried softly.

"Yes." Nate knew she'd have to learn the truth eventually. He thought it better to make a clean break. He just wished she'd back off instead of moving closer.

If Nate had killed a man, he'd been pushed to the limits, and had reacted in self-defense. There was no doubt in her mind. "What did he do to you?" she asked in an anguished whisper.

Nate closed his eyes and ran a hand wearily through his hair. Liana's blind faith in him threatened his control. Nobody had ever cared enough to ask him how he'd felt at the time Buford Harden died.

"Liana tells me that you were with her last night when the accident happened, Harden," the sheriff declared. "Do you want to change your story?"

Nate had no intention of dragging Liana into a mess that could only hurt her. "No," he clipped.

"Nate!" Liana exclaimed, propping her hands on her hips and glaring at him. "Don't do this!"

His response was silence and an unflinching regard. Liana wanted to smack him for being so contrary. She didn't need his protection, and she wasn't going to let him get away with treating her like a Victorian virgin.

She turned her back on Nate and faced the sheriff. "I'm more than willing to take a lie detector test if Mr. Harden refuses to tell the truth. He was with me all night last night."

"I want her name kept out of it," Nate snapped, glaring at Liana and then the sheriff.

"There's no reason to mention Liana if you stick to your original story," the sheriff declared.

"You know his original story is a lie," Liana argued.

"I can't force him to change it."

"Nate!" Liana felt like stamping her feet in frustration. "You had nothing to do with Rod's accident. Why are you letting them do this?"

Nate ignored her question. "How is Rod?"

"He has a severe concussion, and he hasn't regained consciousness," she retorted. "I could be at the hospital with Jamie if you weren't being so hardheaded."

"Go back to the hospital," he commanded tersely. "Let my lawyer worry about the legal problems."

"The problem isn't legal," snapped Liana. "The problem is your refusal to tell the truth."

Nate's eyes narrowed, but he didn't respond.

Liana's frustration increased. She turned to the sheriff as another thought came to mind. "I'll loan my body to your forensic lab," she declared with spirit. "I'm sure there's some physical evidence that Nate and I spent the night together."

"Liana!" Nate ground out her name in shock and anger. He couldn't believe what he was hearing. He started toward her, but she stepped closer to the sheriff's desk and began to unfasten the top buttons of her shirtwaist dress.

"I can probably show you some evidence right here and now," she announced boldly.

"Stop it!" Nate commanded gruffly. He grabbed Liana and turned her to face him. "I don't want you involved," he grated harshly. Then he destroyed his hard-guy image by refastening the buttons on her dress with unsteady fingers.

Liana splayed her hands on the front of his shirt. The hard, familiar warmth of him was reassuring. Her eyes were eloquent and begged him not to shut her out.

"I'm already involved," she insisted urgently, "too involved to be ignored."

Nate wanted to resist the entreaty in her eyes, but he just wasn't strong enough; not when she was so close, not when she touched him. He groaned and closed his eyes as he dragged Liana against his chest.

His arms tightened the instant he felt her body against his. Memories of the previous night flooded through him and made him tremble. He sighed deeply. How could he fight her when she had all the weapons to disarm him?

Nate's eyes were turbulent with emotion as they reopened and locked with Thompson's over Liana's head. The arrogance had dissolved. Now he was torn between the desire to protect her and the desire to be cleared of any charges that could ultimately hurt her.

"Liana's always been a little stubborn," the sheriff declared. "Stubborn and honest."

Nate nodded. He wouldn't label Liana a liar. If she was adamant about making a statement, he wouldn't deny the truth. "I'll file another statement."

Liana slid her arms around Nate's waist and hugged him tightly. He was going to accept her help. She listened to the steady beat of his heart as relief washed over her.

"There's no need to make another statement until your lawyer gets here," said Thompson. "You're still a suspect until we get this thing solved, but Liana's corroboration will make a big difference."

"Can he come with me?" Liana asked as she slowly eased herself from the circle of Nate's arms.

"We're waiting for his lawyer," Thompson explained. "But if you're headed back to the hospital, I'll bring him over there as soon as we're finished."

"Is that okay?" Liana asked Nate. "I can drive you home later." She hoped he wouldn't refuse to speak to her now that she'd made a spectacle of herself.

"It's fine," Nate said. He wondered at her sudden hesitancy. Maybe she was regretting jumping to his defense. "I'd like to see Rod."

The instant she left his arms, Nate reverted to his guarded demeanor. It worried Liana. She hoped he wasn't going to start pushing her away now. "I guess I'll see you both later," she said in the form of a good-bye.

She left the sheriff's department without looking back at anyone. She was beginning to feel like a zombie from emotional stress and lack of sleep.

She went back to the hospital and joined Jamie at Rod's bedside. They spent the next hour talking to the unconscious man, coaxing him to open his eyes.

ELEVEN

Liana's eyes were drooping. She was so sleepy, she could hardly keep her chin off her chest, so she rose from her chair beside Rod's bed and paced the room for a while.

Jamie was equally tired, so the two of them took turns talking to Rod, thinking he might respond more quickly if he could hear their voices. They'd been at it for two hours without any noticeable change in his condition.

The sun was shining brightly outside the window. The hospital grounds were lovely with thick, green grass and several big, old shade trees.

The temperature was still high, but Liana could see a soft breeze fluttering the leaves of the trees. It was a beautiful summer day. A day to be treasured. A day for creating memories. A day for the young and carefree.

She turned abruptly and moved back to Rod's side. Her hand was gentle as she stroked his whisker-stubbled chin, but her voice was firm.

"It's absolutely gorgeous outside," she told the unconscious man. "And here we are cooped up inside this hospital. It's time for you to wake up and get on with your life," she scolded. "Days like this are too rare to let them slip by."

Rod's response was a low moan. It shocked both of the women at his side. They stared at each other and then back at Rod. He was trying to move his head. Another low moan escaped him.

"Rod?" Jamie whispered in an excited tone. "Rod, can you hear me?"

Rod's lips moved, but no sound came. He lifted his eyelids a fraction, dropped them, and then gradually opened his eyes. He licked his lips and tried to speak again.

"What?"

His tone was thick with confusion. Liana knew it was normal to be disoriented, so she tried to explain the situation to him.

"You're at the hospital," she supplied while clasping his hand in hers. Jamie had a firm grip on his other hand. "You had a wreck last night, but the doctors said you're going to be fine."

"I hit a damned tree," he declared hoarsely.

His words brought a rush of tears and trembling smiles to Liana and Jamie. They glanced at each other and then back to their patient.

Rod was slowly pulling himself out of the fog of unconsciousness. "How bad's my car?"

"Totaled." Jamie didn't waste words. "I hope your insurance is up-to-date."

Rod grimaced and then groaned. He eased his hand from Liana's grip and raised it to his head.

When he touched the knot on his forehead, he emitted another moan. "What else did I hit?"

"Your windshield," Liana supplied. "Thank God you were wearing your seat belt or you'd have flown through the window and hit the tree."

"You have a concussion," Jamie told him, "but the doctors said you didn't fracture your skull, and you don't have any internal injuries."

"I feel like I broke every bone in my body."

Liana grinned at him, recaptured his hand, and lifted it to her lips for a kiss. "You're going to be pretty sore for a few days. You're battered and bruised. The human body takes exception to unnecessary abuse. The result is pain."

Rod's lips tilted to smile, then twisted in pain. "I'm getting the message, loud and clear."

"The doctors couldn't give you anything for pain until you recovered consciousness," Jamie explained, her eyes bright with relief and filled with undisguised adoration.

There was a hint of mischief in Rod's eyes as they fastened on Jamie. "A kiss would probably help."

He was going to be all right. Despite his hoarse tone, he sounded normal; wonderfully, wickedly normal. Liana laughed softly, and more tears filled her eyes. Jamie's tears poured down her face as she leaned over to give Rod a kiss.

A nurse entered the room, followed by Sheriff Thompson. Jamie and Liana greeted them, then stepped out of the way while Rod's vital signs were checked.

"Did Nate come with you?" Liana asked the sheriff.

"He's just outside. The nurse wanted to check on Rod before she allowed more company."

"He's doing well," said the nurse as she turned from the bed. "His doctor will be in this afternoon for another checkup, but everything looks fine right now."

"I have to stay here all day?" Rod complained.

Everyone grinned at his impatience. He wasn't in any condition to leave the hospital.

"I can ask him a few questions, can't I?"

The nurse nodded to the sheriff. "He'll have a whopper of a headache for a while, but he can talk as long as he doesn't overdo it," she said.

Liana watched the nurse leave the room and saw Nate in the hallway. She motioned for him to come in the room.

The sheriff greeted Rod warmly and then started asking questions. "Can you tell me what happened last night?"

"From the beginning?" asked Rod.

"As much as you can remember."

Rod licked his lips again. "I got into town late and stopped for gas. Joe Dooms told me that Liana's dad had some serious trouble with his dairy herd, so I decided to drive out there and see if I could help." Jamie stepped close to Rod's side again and offered him a sip of ice water.

"It was almost one when I got to the Banners'. The house was dark except for Liana's room. I tried to be quiet and walked around the house toward her bedroom window."

Rod paused again to catch his breath. Liana was standing at the end of the bed and she felt Nate move closer, but he didn't touch her.

"When I got around the house, I saw Liana and Nate heading across the field toward the woods. I didn't want to yell at them, so I just left."

Rod confirmed Liana's version of Nate's whereabouts, and she uttered a tiny sigh of relief. As long as Rod was sure Nate couldn't have been involved in the wreck, there was no reason for anyone to know the details.

Rod asked Jamie to raise the head of his bed so that he could sit up a little. He winced at the movement, but continued to describe the events of the previous night.

"I headed home, but didn't make it."

"Did you see anyone else on the road while you were driving back?" asked the sheriff.

"I passed Nate's pickup truck about halfway to town," Rod explained. "It was headed toward me."

"But Nate wasn't driving," said Thompson.

Rod nodded, groaned, and then spoke. "It had only been a few minutes since I saw him walking with Liana. It couldn't have been him, but I don't know who was driving. I was tired and not paying that close attention."

"Did the truck turn around and follow you?"

Rod frowned and gave the question some thought. "I guess that's what must have happened. The taillights disappeared, and the next thing I knew, I was being slammed into from behind."

"The pickup truck?"

"Someone had turned off the headlights, so I couldn't get a clear look at the driver, but it was definitely Nate's pickup. It has to look as bad as my car," Rod said in an afterthought, shooting a glance at Nate.

"It's insured," was Nate's only reply, but he managed a smile for Rod.

"You'd better be careful who you let drive your vehicles," Rod suggested.

"It won't happen again." Nate's tone was firm.

"I'd like to get my hands on the jerk that kept slamming into me. What the hell was his purpose? Did he think I was somebody else? Or does someone have a grudge against me that I don't know about?"

Sheriff Thompson shook his head. "We're not sure about motives at this point, but I'd like to know if the driver of the truck was directly responsible for you slamming into that tree."

Rod's brow creased in a frown. "I'm not sure, but I think the truck had backed off, and I was trying to regain control. It all happened so fast."

"The truck didn't actually shove you into the tree?"

"I don't think so," Rod said with a frown. "I'm sorry I can't be more help."

"You've done fine," said Thompson. "I have all the information I need right now. Just take care of yourself, and we'll talk again when you're feeling better."

The sheriff said good-bye to everyone and left the room. Liana moved to Rod's side again and gave him a brief kiss. "I'm going to leave and take Nate with me. You need to get some rest and have the doctor give you something for that headache. I'll be back this evening."

"You're the one who'd better get some rest," Rod commented. "You look ready to drop."

Liana knew he was right, but ignored his scolding.

"I won't tell you what you look like," she teased lightly. "But I trust Jamie to make you behave."

Rod gave her a weary smile. He and Nate exchanged a few words, and then Liana led the way out of the hospital to the parking lot.

"What are you driving?"

"Mother's Chevy," Liana replied, pointing to where she'd parked the car.

"I'll drive."

She didn't argue, just fished the keys out of her purse and handed them to Nate. He opened the passenger door when they reached the car, and Liana slid into the seat. She noticed that he was being careful not to touch her.

The interior of the car was hot and stuffy. Nate started the engine and turned on the air conditioning to make Liana comfortable. She looked as if she was ready to collapse, and he blamed himself for her exhaustion.

He shouldn't have gone to her house last night. He should have resisted the temptation to spend time with her. The withdrawal would have been so much easier if he hadn't tasted the sweetness of her responses; if he hadn't been so completely enthralled by her exquisite beauty.

Liana was a very beautiful woman; not just in looks, but in heart and spirit. He'd never wanted a woman more, nor felt less worthy of a woman's love and loyalty.

Liana's eyes were closed as she rested her head on the back of the seat. "Have you decided it's safer not to speak to me or touch me?" she asked tiredly.

Nate shot her a quick glance and then turned his attention back to the road. "It's a lot safer for you."

"And what if I'm sick and tired of being safe?" Liana demanded irritably. "What if I'm sick and tired of people telling me they know what's best for me? What if I don't like the way you tried to protect me? What if I don't like your fierce denial of the time you spent with me?"

Nate's hands clenched around the steering wheel. "What we shared was private and nobody else's business," he stated flatly. "It shouldn't have happened."

Liana turned shocked eyes on him. "You don't really believe that!" she cried in disbelief.

When he didn't rescind his declaration, her voice softened. She hoped to penetrate the invisible barrier he was erecting. "I love you, Nate."

"No!" Nate's denial was harsh. He dragged in a rough breath as her words threatened his control. "You don't love me," he snapped. "You love the way I make you feel. There's a hell of a lot of difference."

Liana's chest tightened with emotion. "Are you trying to tell me that what we shared was just physical? That it would be the same with any partner, and that you don't have any special feelings for me?"

Nate couldn't force a deliberate lie past his throat, so he left her questions unanswered. "What I'm saying is that it was great, but it's finished."

"Because you got what you wanted from me, and now it's time to find a new playmate?"

She was the only woman who had ever managed to tie him in knots with just a few words. "Dammit, Liana, don't say things like that!" he ground out roughly. "I wasn't looking for a one-night stand, and I'm not demeaning what we shared. There's just no future for us."

"Why?"

"Why?" he repeated angrily. "You know why."

"I honestly don't," she told him quietly.

Nate couldn't find the words to describe his insecurities, and he didn't want to think about all the reasons they were unsuited for each other.

A silence taut with tension filled the car for the rest of the way to Liana's house. She was the first to speak as Nate turned in to her driveway.

"Why did you bring me home first?"

"I want to talk to your dad, and I can walk home."

Liana didn't say anything, just climbed from the car before Nate had a chance to offer assistance. Her back was rigid and her head high as she preceded him to the house.

Gloria met them at the door. "How's Rod?"

Liana stopped on the porch and managed a smile for her mother. "He's conscious and already complaining about staying at the hospital. He should be fine in a few days."

"Thank God!" said Gloria, her face crinkling in a smile. Then she turned to Nate. "Your mother was here a few minutes ago. She and your cousin arrived at the house and couldn't find you, so she came here. She was going to town, but I suggested she go back to the house until we heard from you. You're welcome to use my car."

"Thanks," said Nate. "I'd better get over there before she gets too worried. Tell Dave I'll catch him later when I return your car."

Gloria nodded and turned her eyes back to Liana.

"I know, I know," Liana groused. "I need a nap! I always need a nap! I'm going straight to bed."

It was as good an excuse as she could find for not looking at, or speaking to, Nate. She entered the house without a backward glance. Then she climbed the stairs, went into her room, and collapsed on the bed, exhausted. Her shoes and purse hit the floor, but she had no energy to undress. She was asleep in minutes.

The shirtwaist dress was wrinkled and clinging to her damp skin when Liana awakened in the late afternoon. She lay still for a few minutes and recalled every detail of the morning's events.

Even though Nate had been cleared of suspicion in Rod's wreck, she knew he wanted to put an end to their relationship. It hurt. Badly. And it frightened her.

She'd never been so overwhelmed by emotions. She'd loved Rod, but her feelings for him were shallow compared to the intensity of her love for Nate. They'd only known each other for a few weeks, yet there wasn't a doubt in her mind or heart that they were meant for each other.

She couldn't let him destroy their future. She couldn't give him time to erect more barriers between them. If he thought the knowledge of his criminal record would make a difference in how she felt, then he was badly mistaken.

Liana wished he would tell her the whole story and share his feelings, but it didn't matter. She loved him, unequivocally, desperately, achingly. She wanted to be in his arms and hold him until he admitted he felt the same.

Of course, there was a chance that he didn't love her. Liana's breathing faltered at the thought. Maybe she was just another in a long line of women. She'd given Nate her heart and body last night. Maybe he hadn't felt the same. He hadn't said anything about the future or commitment.

Liana couldn't let herself dwell on the possibility that Nate didn't love her. He hadn't said the words, but he had to feel something special or they couldn't have shared such uninhibited loving. If his love wasn't as strong as hers, then she'd have to work on strengthening whatever feelings he had.

One thing was certain, she thought as she rose from bed and began to undress. She wasn't going to act like a shrinking violet. She knew what she wanted, and she was willing to fight for it. Nate Harden didn't stand a chance.

Liana showered, washed her hair, and redressed in a mint green outfit of knit walking shorts and a sleeveless pullover shirt. She brushed her hair until it crackled and let it hang down her back. Then she headed downstairs to find her mother.

The delicious aromas wafting from the kitchen reminded her that she hadn't eaten anything all day. Her stomach growled at the thought, and Liana gave her mother a wide smile when she entered the kitchen.

"Something smells wonderful, and I'm starving."

"I imagine you are, sweetheart," Gloria replied as she shared a brief hug with her daughter. "You look rested and much better than you did a few hours ago."

"I feel better," was Liana's reply. She noticed that the table was set for six people. "Are we having company?"

"I invited Olive, Peter, and Nate to join us for

dinner. I didn't want them to worry about cooking a meal this evening.''

"That's nice," said Liana. She was anxious to meet Nate's mother and cousin. She also wanted to see Nate.

"What can I do to help?"

Gloria put her to work, and the two of them discussed the day's events while preparing their meal. Liana told her mother as much as she could without divulging the details of her night with Nate. She hesitated about mentioning his criminal record, but Gloria had already heard rumors.

"I've had several calls today warning me to be careful around Nate." Gloria snorted indignantly. "I gave a few people a piece of my mind, too. I can't stop the gossip, but I'm a perfectly good judge of character, and if Nate killed a man, it must have been in self-defense.''

Unexpected tears rushed to Liana's eyes. Her mother's faith in Nate made her feel weepy, and relieved, and proud. She put down the dish she was holding and wrapped her arms around her mother. "Thank you," was all she could say.

Liana's sudden burst of emotion momentarily surprised Gloria. She returned her hug, then drew back and brushed some strands of hair over her daughter's shoulders.

"I know you care for Nate, too," Gloria said. "But maybe you'd better tell me just how much you care.''

Liana wiped away her tears and managed a smile. "I'm madly in love with him. Does that surprise you?''

Gloria scrutinized her daughter more carefully. "I

knew there was a strong attraction between the two of you," she admitted. "You haven't known Nate very long, but true love can't be measured by time. I just don't want you to confuse compassion for love."

Liana laughed softly. She didn't lack confidence in her feelings. "It would be a relief to only feel compassion."

"You don't want to be in love with Nate?"

"Loving Nate and convincing him that he loves me might be the hardest things I've ever done in my life."

Gloria returned to meal preparations. "Nate's determined to protect you from the gossip, isn't he?"

"He wants to keep his distance."

"What are you going to do about it?"

"I'm not letting him get away with it," Liana said with feeling. "I refuse to be set aside like some fragile doll. I love him, and I don't care what people think. They don't know him like I do, and he's not likely to give them the chance to know him. But I'm more than willing to fight for him, whether he likes it or not."

Liana's heated declaration ended with the sound of the door opening. She turned from the cupboard and saw her dad ushering a young man and older woman into the kitchen.

A blush rose to her cheeks when she realized that their guests had heard her little tirade. They had to be Nate's family, but he was nowhere in sight.

"Olive and Peter," said Dave. "I'd like you to meet our daughter, Liana."

Olive looked like the portrait Liana had found in Nate's attic, except that her ebony hair was streaked with gray, and the lines of age on her face declared the passing of time. Her eyes, however, were sparkling.

Olive didn't even say hello. She just held out her arms and asked, "May I give a hug to this lovely woman who defends my son so fiercely?"

Liana went into Olive's arms and hugged her tightly. The older woman didn't resemble her son in the least, but Liana liked being close to her simply because she was important to Nate.

"Hey, what about me?"

The two women slowly withdrew their arms from each other. The smile they shared was filled with warmth.

"This is my nephew, Peter," said Olive. "He gets jealous when I get all the hugs."

Liana laughed and smiled at Peter. He was shorter than Nate, and darkly handsome. His looks favored Olive's Greek ancestry more than Nate's did, but Liana knew there was no blood relation between the two of them.

She held out a hand in greeting and then laughed when Peter groaned. "Why does Olive always get the hugs, and I get a handshake?"

TWELVE

Liana removed one place setting from the table. Olive had made Nate's excuses. He'd said the day had been so hectic that he needed to catch up on his work. She was disappointed, but not discouraged.

It was a pleasure to get to know Olive and Peter. They were both charming, and conversation was lively throughout dinner. Olive had done a great deal of traveling, and Peter proclaimed himself her devoted companion. The two of them shared stories of their travels.

Olive and Gloria had done some visiting earlier in the day, but they continued to renew their friendship. Everyone was enjoying dessert and coffee before the conversation turned serious.

"Nate chose not to join us for dinner," Olive began, "so I'm going to take the opportunity to tell you a little about him. He never talks about his past, and I feel you all have the right to know the truth. Has he mentioned his stepfather to any of you?" she asked.

Gloria's response was negative. Nate had told Dave that Buford Harden was a good farmer. Liana was slow to respond. She looked directly at Olive, and wondered what she could say that wouldn't betray Nate's confidence.

"I know he hated Buford," Olive supplied to convince her it was no family secret. "I just don't know how much he's explained."

"He said he was thirteen before he learned that Buford wasn't his real father," Liana volunteered hesitantly.

Their guests' expressions registered total amazement. Peter gasped. Olive's mouth dropped open, and her dark eyes grew misty. Liana immediately regretted saying anything.

Olive swiped a hand over her eyes and apologized. "I'm sorry, Liana, you took us by surprise."

"Nate never discusses his past," Peter explained. "I didn't even know he believed Buford was his real father."

"I knew," put in Olive. "Buford and I agreed to keep Nate's illegitimacy a secret, but I thought Nate was almost sixteen before he learned the truth. He must have known it years before I told him."

Olive had grown pale, and Liana knew she was imagining the mental torture her dead husband might have inflicted on Nate for years before she was aware of it.

"I'm really sorry, Olive. I thought you knew or I wouldn't have said anything. Nate will be furious."

"Nate has protected me far too long already," Olive insisted spiritedly. "I hate to think what he's suffered to protect me. I won't have it anymore!"

Liana smiled. She could understood how Olive

felt, but she didn't think there was much chance of reforming Nate.

Gloria poured everyone another cup of coffee, and Olive continued her explanation of the past. "When Buford died, I had a mental and emotional breakdown. I had to be hospitalized for nearly a year, and I wasn't there for Nate when he needed me most."

Her voice broke, but she quickly regained control. "Nate was tried for manslaughter, and spent months in jail. He was found guilty, but the judge was lenient. He gave Nate the opportunity to join the army, and he did.

"I inherited Buford's estate, and Peter's father handled my affairs until I was recovered. Then I sold all of Buford's property and became a very wealthy woman, but Nate would never take a penny from me. He worked like a madman to build his own empire, and I've always been very proud of him."

Nate's refusal to use Buford Harden's money didn't surprise Liana. He was a proud man, and the money rightfully belonged to his mother. He was probably more concerned about her emotional and financial independence.

"For many years we put the past behind us and never spoke of Buford," Olive continued. "Peter and I made our home with Nate, and we were doing fine. Then I started getting nightmares. Nate insisted I see a doctor, and I agreed to undergo hypnosis."

Olive's hand trembled as she carefully placed her coffee cup on the saucer. Peter reached over and clasped her hand in support.

"Olive, please, if the memories are too painful, don't worry about telling us right now. There'll be plenty of time later," Gloria insisted.

Olive was shaking her head, and her expression was fierce. "It's been too long already," she declared. "The therapist said I need to come to terms with the truth."

"Would you like me to tell the rest?" asked Peter.

Olive was shaking her head again. "While my mind was sick, I couldn't remember what happened the night Buford died," she said, "but when I really began to heal, the memories began to surface. I relived those hours in my dreams, and later through hypnosis. I learned that Nate wasn't the one who killed Buford. I did."

Gloria gasped and reached a hand out to her friend in comfort. Dave was equally amazed and sympathetic. Liana was the least surprised. Her heart had never accepted the fact that Nate would kill someone. She was only sorry that he hadn't trusted her enough to tell her the whole truth.

"He never told anyone?" asked Dave.

"Not even his lawyers, or me when I got stronger," Olive told them. "If I hadn't remembered, he would have carried the burden of my guilt for the rest of his life."

"I don't imagine he was very happy when you remembered," Liana surmised.

"I begged him to let me take my knowledge to court so that his name could be cleared. Buford was beating me that night and knocked me to the floor. I grabbed a poker and struck back for the first time in eighteen years. I knew the courts would understand that I reacted in self-defense, but Nate absolutely refused to consider reopening the case."

"I can understand his reluctance," commented Dave. "It wouldn't have done any good to stir up the memories. It would have threatened the new life you'd made, and put your future at risk."

"I understood the risks involved," said Olive, "but I feared exactly what happened here today. All Nate wants is to have a home and land he can farm. I don't want that jeopardized. I don't want him punished for protecting me."

"I don't think there's much choice in the matter," said Liana. She wondered if she would ever stop aching for Nate. His broad shoulders had carried some heavy burdens, and it was no wonder that his wounded heart was wary.

When all eyes turned to her, she explained, "Nate is a man who protects his own. Like it or not, if you love him and he loves you, he's going to be possessive and protective. He probably doesn't even know how to be selfish."

Olive sighed heavily. "I'm just so sorry this had to happen here in Springdale," she told them. "I wanted to make a new start and avoid the gossip. Instead, I'm responsible for the damage being done to my son's reputation."

"You're not entirely responsible," Dave said. He told Olive about the other attempts to discredit Nate: the poisoning of his herd and Rod's accident. "Someone doesn't want Nate to settle in Springdale," he concluded.

"Do you think it has anything to do with Uncle Buford's death?" asked Peter.

"I doubt it," Liana replied. "Nobody knew about that until Nate was arrested this morning."

"You don't think Jay's family is harboring a grudge, do you?" asked Olive.

Dave and Gloria both shook their heads. "The

Newsome family is outspoken and honest. If they had a problem, they'd be straightforward about it," said Dave.

"Then who?" Gloria wondered aloud.

"I hope that's what the sheriff's trying to find out," Liana told her. "So far, nobody's having much luck."

"Do you think it would help if I talked to the sheriff?" asked Olive.

"It couldn't hurt," Gloria told her friend. "Maybe you can offer some insight about your father that will help the investigation. He and his property have to be at the root of the problem."

"I'll talk to him first thing in the morning," Olive declared. "And while I'm at it, I fully intend to explain that my son is not a criminal."

"If you see a deputy named Rondel, you might want to thank him for spreading the gossip," suggested Liana.

"Rondel?" queried Olive. She'd grown accustomed to the power of her wealth over the past few years. Maybe it was time to throw her weight around in Springdale. She wasn't a frightened, pregnant teenager anymore. "I'll remember that name."

Liana smiled as she caught a nuance in Olive's voice that reminded her of Nate. It wasn't hard to see where he got his strength of character. Olive had suffered years of debilitating abuse, yet she'd managed to fight back and recover her self-respect. Now she had new purpose in her life.

"Are you planning to go back to the hospital this evening?" Gloria asked Liana.

Liana nodded. "I want to see Rod again and make sure Jamie gets out of the hospital for a little while."

"Then why don't you go ahead," Gloria insisted. "I can take care of the dishes."

"I'll be happy to help your mother," said Olive. "We haven't giggled over our chores for more years than I care to count."

The two women exchanged smiles and immediately began to clear the table. "You can take my car," said Gloria. "Nate brought it back with a full tank of gas and parked it out front. The keys are on the telephone stand."

Dave had already invited Peter on a tour of the farm, so Liana excused herself to go to the hospital. She grabbed her purse and the keys, then headed for town.

When she entered Rod's room fifteen minutes later, she was greeted by hugs and kisses from both his parents. His dad, Gary, was an older version of Rod's tall, dark, and handsome. His mother, Marti, was tall, slim, and attractive.

"It's good to see you," Liana exclaimed. "I'm sorry your vacation got cut so short, but Rod had us a little worried this morning."

"I think Gary broke every speed limit all the way home," said Marti. "I've never been so scared in my life."

Rod grumbled that they shouldn't have hurried home. He thought he was perfectly all right and should be released from the hospital.

"The nurses just want to keep you because you're so cute," Liana teased him as she gave him a kiss. "You might as well take advantage of all this attention."

"You'd change your tune if you had to eat the food they served for supper," Rod growled. "And

I've lost count of the times they've poked and jabbed me.''

Their laughter didn't improve his temperament.

"Where's Jamie? Did you run her off?" asked Liana.

"I sent the poor girl home to rest and take a break," said Marti. "She was beat, and Mr. Congeniality was beginning to upset her."

"Rod!"

"Don't start," he snapped. "I've had a helluva rotten day, and I didn't mean to take it out on her. I'll apologize as soon as she gets back. If she comes back."

Liana knew he was regretting his ill temper, and that he was worried about Jamie, so she changed the subject. She told him about Olive and Peter having dinner at her house.

"Are they nice people?" Marti asked. "Nate seems a nice man. He sent an insurance agent to assess damages on Rod's car, and he was willing to take care of all the hospital bills, as well."

"Not that I'm going to let him," injected Rod. "I have insurance, and he's not responsible for this mess."

Liana grinned at his defensiveness and wondered if his ego wasn't a bit bruised. She tried distracting him with small talk. "Olive and Peter seem really nice," she told them. "They've done a lot of traveling and have some really interesting stories to tell."

"Do you think they'll stay in Springdale?" Marti asked.

"That's their plan. I guess they make their home wherever Nate is, but I can't imagine them being content to spend all their time here."

The door to Rod's room opened and Jamie stuck her head in before entering. She gave Liana a grin, but her expression wasn't as pleasant when she turned to Rod.

"Is the patient feeling any less aggressive?"

"The patient is fine," snapped Rod. Then, after a reproving glance from Liana, he managed a half smile for Jamie. "I promise it's safe to be in the same room with me."

"Cross your heart?" Jamie taunted.

Rod frowned in irritation, and Liana thought it might be a good time to leave. "I have to be going now."

Gary and Marti hadn't eaten dinner, so they decided to go for a meal while Jamie was with Rod. Liana left the room with them, then parted ways in the parking lot.

She was going to Nate's house.

Dusk had fallen by the time she pulled to a stop behind Nate's car in his driveway. The house was dark, but that didn't dampen her determination. She would check the house first, then scour every inch of the farm, if necessary.

Liana had to see Nate. She had to talk to him and touch him. She only felt half-alive when they were apart. It was insane. Her need to be near him was unreasonable, yet it couldn't be denied.

Nate had given her a key, but Liana didn't have to use it. The door was unlocked, and she didn't hesitate to enter. She'd grown to love the house more each day she worked in it, and felt perfectly at home here.

After closing the door behind her, Liana called Nate's name softly, but got no response. She repeated the process in every room; calling to Nate, turning lights on and then off again as she moved through the downstairs.

When a search of the first floor didn't produce her quarry, Liana headed upstairs to the master bedroom. She thought it unlikely that Nate had retired for the night, but he might not have heard her if he was in the shower.

There was no light under the bedroom door, but when Liana got closer, she heard music. Her knock went unheard, so she opened the door and called Nate again. Her eyes were accustomed to the darkness, so she found him immediately.

As soon as Nate caught sight of her, he touched the remote control on his bedside stand and lowered the volume of his stereo. The music softened, and there was just enough light in the room for them to see each other clearly.

Liana closed the door behind her and leaned against it for support. Finding Nate stretched out on his bed in nothing but denim shorts was a shock to her sensory system. He was so gorgeous and so incredibly sexy that he stole her breath. She felt sharp, piercing desire at the sight of him, and trembled with the need to touch and be touched. It was an effort to control the violent trembling of her limbs.

Just the sight of her aroused Nate. His muscles knotted, and his body grew hard and tight with need. It didn't help that he'd spent the last two hours reliving every minute of their night together. It didn't help that she was so beautiful, and that she had come to his bedroom.

For a long moment they just drank in the sight of each other. Tension vibrated between them like a physical force. Liana tried to control her shallow, ragged breathing.

Nate heard the blood pounding in his head. He'd promised himself he wouldn't let her know how desperately he needed her, but it was hard to hide so raw a hunger.

His eyes scoured her every feature. Her eyes were dark with the same tumultuous emotions he was experiencing. Her hair fell over her shoulders like a soft, shimmering cloak. He clenched his fingers to still the itch to touch, and his mouth tightened at the thought of kissing every inch of her satin skin.

"You shouldn't have come," Nate managed to growl through clenched teeth.

"I had to," Liana explained huskily. Her eyes beseeched him not to reject her need to be with him. Her heart was pounding so violently that she could hardly speak. She hadn't moved a muscle since entering the room, and she silently pleaded for some sign that he really cared.

Nate finally looked away from her and raked his hands through his hair in frustration. He couldn't stand the vulnerability in her eyes. He had to make her understand that they couldn't have a future. It was better to end it here and now.

"Last night was a mistake." He got the words out, but he couldn't look her in the eyes when he said them. "I feel like a heel for making love to you just to satisfy a temporary need. All I can say is I'm sorry."

His apology cut like a knife. Liana felt the crushing weight of his rejection, and struggled to understand. "Did I do something wrong?" she asked in trembling tones.

Nate was off the bed and beside her before she'd caught her breath. "It's not your fault!" he snarled. "You didn't do anything wrong!"

Liana tilted her head slightly so that she could look him in the eyes. He was standing so close, she could feel the heat of his body, but neither of them reached out to touch the other.

"Everything's always your fault, isn't it, Nate?" she accused softly. "When are you going to stop carrying the weight of the world on your shoulders? Are you ever going to let anyone share the responsibility for matters beyond your control?"

"This is not beyond my control."

Liana's laugh was a strangled sound. "Then you're a hell of a lot stronger than I am," she whispered roughly, "because what I feel for you is totally beyond my control."

Nate made a rough sound in his throat. He clenched his jaws tightly and balled his hands into fists to keep from reaching for her. He could bear his own pain, but hers could swiftly destroy his defenses.

"It's all wrong, Liana." His past would always get in the way of a serious commitment. His chosen life-style was one that she was hell-bent to escape.

She shook her head slowly from side to side. "Touch me and say that," she challenged. She was still pressed against the door, waiting for him to welcome any move she might make. "Hold me and tell me the way we feel about each other is wrong."

The only way to convince her that there was no future for them was to convince her that he didn't want her in his life. Nate knew what to do. He'd done it before, he just didn't know if he was capable of pulling it off with Liana.

He stepped closer, and his pulse accelerated. She smelled sweet and sexy. Her eyes were bright, her lips softly parted, and her body was taut with anticipation. The tension between them was so heavy, it felt as if they were touching before he lifted a hand.

"Don't bother trying to intimidate me or trying to scare me off with some rough handling," Liana warned, sensing Nate's mood. "You might have used those tactics in the past, but they won't work with me. I really love you, and I trust the man behind the facade."

Nate closed his eyes on a moan. It took every ounce of his physical strength to keep from dragging her into his arms. He wanted to be reasonable and explain the logic of his decision, but they couldn't have a serious conversation in his bedroom. He needed to get Liana out of here.

The pregnant silence was unexpectedly interrupted by the sound of someone climbing the staircase. Nate and Liana both stiffened as they heard the creaking of each stair step.

"Did anyone come with you?" he asked softly.

"No. Your mother and Peter planned to spend the whole evening with my parents," she whispered.

Nobody else should have been in the house. There was something sinister in the sound of the slow creak of each stair. Someone was being very cautious. Nate and Liana's eyes locked, both pairs registering suspicion. He motioned for her to move away from the door, and she did, then watched over his shoulder as he cracked it slightly.

The hallway was dark. The intruder obviously

hadn't turned on lights. All they could see was an outline of a man carrying something. He headed for the door of the stairway to the top floor. Nate started to close the bedroom door, but then they both caught the scent of gasoline.

"He's going to torch the house!" Nate rasped. He swore violently and warned Liana. "Get out of here as fast as you can!" he commanded as he flung open his door and raced down the hall.

"Nate, don't! I'll call for help!" she cried in a rough whisper.

He didn't slow down or look back. Liana knew she couldn't stop him from protecting his home. She found his bedroom phone and called 911, telling the dispatcher that there was an emergency need for the fire department and sheriff. Then she followed Nate.

He was out of sight on the top floor, and she started to follow when she heard the unmistakable whooshing sound of a gasoline explosion.

Liana screamed and opened the door to the second stairway. She was hit with a wave of gas fumes and immediately backed away from the door. She could hear the crackle of flames, and feared the fire department would be too late to save the house. Then she remembered a fire extinguisher that she'd seen stored in the utility room.

In a matter of minutes she had dashed down the staircase, run through the house, and raced back up the stairs with the portable extinguisher. She was panting and breathless as she rushed to the second set of stairs.

As she reached to open the door, a body came hurtling down the steps. Liana screamed again and dodged the tumbling body. It took only a glance to realize that the body wasn't Nate's, so she stepped over the motionless form and headed up the narrow staircase.

The smoke was getting thick in the attic loft, but Liana could see Nate battling the fire with a large throw rug. The arsonist had doused the furniture in the middle of the room with gasoline, and Nate was trying to minimize the flames by suffocating them.

She yelled his name to get his attention and then began to cough from the combination of shortness of breath and acrid smoke filling her lungs.

"Get out of here!" Nate yelled, his eyes widening with fear for her safety.

"Extinguisher!" she shouted. Unfortunately, she didn't know how to use it.

Nate was beside her in an instant. He grabbed the tank, adjusted the valve, and pointed the nozzle toward the flaming pile of furniture. He ordered her to leave, but she stayed. Then they heard the approaching sound of sirens.

"Help them, and then stay clear of the house!"

This time Liana obeyed. Her eyes were watering, and her breathing was harsh. Her lungs were burning like fire, but she found the strength to run down the stairs and out of the house as the first firemen swung off the truck.

"Where's the fire?"

"The top floor," she shouted, coughing again.

"How widespread is it?"

"It's in the attic. Nate's fighting it with an extinguisher, but the smoke's the worst."

The firemen nodded and headed inside with some of their own equipment. Another crew started to position a ladder near the windows of the top story. Liana pointed to the area closest to the fire.

A medic tried to put an oxygen mask over her face, but she brushed him aside as she saw Sheriff Thompson's cruiser pull to a stop. She ran to meet him.

"What's happened?" asked Thompson as he and a deputy joined her.

"Someone poured gasoline on the furniture stored in the attic, but the fire's confined to the third floor," she explained as they headed into the house. "Nate must have overpowered the guy, because he's unconscious," she added as they climbed the stairs.

One of the firemen was bending over Ned Larkin as they reached the second floor. All the lights were ablaze now. Liana hadn't recognized Ned in the darkness, but the sight of him suddenly made all the pieces of the puzzle fall together. Larkin was responsible for Nate's recent problems.

The farm manager began swearing as soon as he regained consciousness. A fireman warned him not to move, but Ned shoved him aside and rose to his feet. He staggered, leaned against the wall for support, and glared at Liana.

The instant he started hurling obscenities at her, the sheriff and deputy started reading him his rights. They grabbed him by both arms, restrained him with handcuffs, and led him down the stairs. Sheriff Thompson told Liana to follow, but she ignored him.

She needed to make sure Nate was all right. It did little good for the fireman to issue another warning as she climbed the second staircase.

The air wasn't nearly so suffocating now. The fire

had been extinguished and windows had been opened to allow fresh air into the loft. Most of the smoke was clearing.

Liana's eyes flew to Nate. He saw her at the same time. In a matter of seconds, she was in his arms.

_____ THIRTEEN _____

"I guess Ned Larkin worked for Mr. Drenasis all those years because he thought the old man would eventually leave the farm to him," explained Sheriff Thompson.

"But Drenasis drew up a will that left everything to his daughter," he continued. "Ned and another employee signed the will as witnesses, making it legal. Then Ned promised the old man he'd take it to town and have it recorded. I guess Drenasis trusted him and didn't bother to find out if it was filed at the court house."

Liana and Nate were spending their evening the same way they'd spent the morning: in the sheriff's office. Dave and Gloria, and Olive and Peter, were also present. They were all seated around the sheriff's desk.

"Did Ned confess everything?" asked Dave.

"He wouldn't say a thing until we got a search warrant for his house and found a copy of the will.

Then he started raving like a madman and told us everything.''

''He was stupid to keep the evidence,'' put in Peter.

The sheriff nodded. ''Ned's not the brightest criminal I've ever come across. If he'd destroyed the will he'd have had one less charge against him, and we wouldn't have a motive for the other charges. Now we'll have the evidence to make the charges stick.''

''What about the employee who co-signed?'' asked Olive.

''He still lives in the area, but he's on disability and doesn't work anymore. When I questioned him, he said he remembered Ned asking him to sign some papers, but he didn't understand the importance of it.''

''So my father really decided to leave his property to me?'' Olive asked in a thin voice.

Liana knew Nate's mother had been badly frightened when she learned about the fire. She was still very pale, but composed. It was difficult to gauge her reaction to learning about her father's change of heart.

''Seems like it,'' said Thompson. ''I know there'll be a legal hassle to get everything straightened out, but the will looks valid.''

''Ned must have been furious when Nate bought the property,'' Dave commented.

''He had hoped to coerce Drenasis into making another will before he died, but the old man's death was too sudden. Ned decided his only recourse was to scare off the new owners,'' Thompson explained. ''He's confessed to poisoning your herd, running

Rod off the road, and several other incidents that occurred at the farm.''

"What did he hope to accomplish?" asked Nate. He was exhausted, but still furious over Larkin's actions and the damage his maniacal behavior had done to his mother, his neighbors, and especially his relationship with Liana. "Even if he'd managed to run me off, he couldn't afford the place himself."

"He has a considerable amount of money invested in bonds that are due to mature later this year," said Thompson. "He figured he could come up with enough money for a down payment by the time you offered the place for sale."

Liana was shaking her head in disbelief. "The property still wouldn't have been rightfully his," she insisted. "It belongs to Olive and Nate."

"He thought he was safe. He had the only evidence of Drenasis' last will."

"And didn't destroy it," reiterated Peter. "It's hard to believe that anyone could be that stupid."

"He was obsessed about that property, but not very smart," agreed the sheriff. "I think he felt secure as long as he had the will in his possession."

"Well, I certainly hope it's all over now," Gloria declared emphatically. "We've had about all the excitement we can stand for a while."

"It's a mighty good thing that you were at home tonight, Nate," added Dave, "or the whole place might have gone up in flames. Ned must have been getting desperate."

Nate and Liana were still covered with smoke and soot from the fire. As soon as it had been safe to leave, they'd come to the sheriff's office to give their statements. A few firemen and a cleaning crew were still working at the house.

"I'm just glad it wasn't more serious," said Nate.

The fire had been put out with extinguishers, so there wasn't any water damage. Most of the flames had been confined to the pile of furniture, and the smoke damage was limited to the third floor.

"The fire chief doesn't think there's any structural damage," he added, "and none of the remodeling was affected."

"The gasoline didn't have long enough to soak into the wood before the fire was ignited. That's why it was easier to get control of," Dave surmised.

"All those beautiful antiques!" Liana moaned. Her voice was husky from inhaling so much smoke. Her eyes met Nate's, and his briefly darkened with anger before going completely devoid of emotion. He hadn't said a word to her since he'd dragged her out of his house, hugged her until she couldn't breathe, and chastised her for risking her life.

"We did save some of them," Olive told her in a comforting tone. "Peter and I looked through them this afternoon, and we moved a few smaller pieces downstairs, including my portrait."

Liana gave Nate's mother a tired smile. "I'm glad."

"It might be possible to salvage more," put in Peter. "Some of the pieces on the bottom of the pile were protected. Some of the others were just surface-damaged."

Liana gave Peter a smile, too. He seemed genuinely interested in the aesthetic value of the furnishings that Nate had been determined not to use. She'd learned that Peter made a hobby of refurbishing antique furniture.

"Maybe we'll put you to work on some of the final remodeling projects," Liana declared.

"No way," returned Peter. "Not after seeing the quality and style of your work. I'm too much of an amateur."

Liana laughed softly and shook her head at his flattery. She'd decided she really liked Peter. He was friendly and good natured.

"What happens next?" Nate asked the sheriff. His tone was terse. He didn't like the way Peter's eyes sparkled when he looked at Liana, and he didn't like the smile in her voice when she spoke to his cousin.

"Ned will be incarcerated until the preliminary hearing. He's signed a written confession, so he'll probably be sentenced to several years in prison."

"Such a shame," Gloria proclaimed.

"That it is," replied the sheriff.

"Do you need anything else tonight?" asked Nate.

"No, you can all go home and relax now," Thompson told them. "I know it's been a long day."

Nate rose from his chair and offered the sheriff his hand. "Thanks for your help."

All the others offered their thanks and farewells as they filed out of the office. In the parking lot, they headed for two separate cars. Nate said a gruff good night, then climbed behind the wheel of his mother's car. Liana had little choice but to go home with her parents.

It was past eleven o'clock when the Banners arrived home. Dave and Gloria went straight to bed. Liana headed for the shower. She stripped off her filthy clothes and scrubbed herself until she felt clean again. Then she collapsed onto her own bed and slept.

A crowing rooster awakened her just before dawn the next morning. She felt rested, but restless. Her dreams had been filled with troubling images of Nate. Her heart ached with love for him and the need to share that love.

Nothing between them had been resolved. He'd been furious with her for not getting herself out of a dangerous situation and staying out of harm's way. She'd been equally furious at him for suggesting that she run and protect herself when he'd desperately needed help.

Except for one crushing hug of relief, he hadn't touched her all evening. Except for yelling at her, he hadn't said much. He hadn't even wanted to look at her.

Liana alternately considered never speaking to him again, or confronting him and demanding a confession of love. She couldn't decide which course of action was the best for both of them. Should she just let him walk out of her life, or should she fight for his love?

One thing for sure, she didn't feel like going downstairs and discussing the events of last night with her mother. Soon the phone would be ringing off the hook, and she wasn't ready to answer more questions about the fire. All she wanted was some time to think, and to see Nate.

As she had done many times over the years, Liana dressed quietly and slipped out her bedroom window. She headed for the artesian pool on Nate's property to search her head and heart for resolutions. It was the one place where she felt completely at peace with the world.

Her dad was already in the barn when she passed that way, but he didn't notice her. Smokey was fully recovered from his illness, but she was glad he didn't see her as she crossed her dad's property to the woods.

It was another warm, balmy summer day, with birds singing from every tree. Liana loved the sound of turtle doves cooing to each other. Their song always soothed her with memories of a happy, carefree childhood.

She breathed deeply, enjoying the sweet smell of freshly cut alfalfa hay. How she loved it. There was so much she loved about her home. How could she have let her career ambitions deprive her of the very basic pleasures in life?

Her work was important to her. It always would be. She'd thought the only way to have a successful career was to work in a major city. Working for Nate had proven otherwise.

None of her upscale projects in New York had ever given her the kind of satisfaction she'd found in remodeling Nate's home. Part of the reason was due to her love of his house and her fascination with its owner. But a large part was due to the challenge of creating a home that was both elegant and comfortable.

She'd never seriously considered working in Ohio and living close to home. At least, she hadn't until she'd met Nate. Now she was considering a variety of possibilities and giving the idea plenty of thought.

When Liana reached the fence that separated his property from her dad's, she looked toward the pond, and her heart skipped a beat. Nate was there. He was shirtless and stepping out of his jeans and briefs.

His chest, shoulder, and back muscles rippled with every movement, and her breathing faltered. She watched, totally enthralled, as his beautifully sculpted nude body moved to the edge of the pond and cut into the water with power and agility.

The muscles in her stomach coiled into a tight knot. Excitement rippled through her as well as a fierce longing for the man who had shown her so much passion and tenderness. She had to force herself to relax and quietly shorten the distance between them.

At the boulders, Liana recovered the clothing Nate had shed and folded everything neatly across the rocks. When she felt as though she had herself in control again, she turned admiring eyes on the gorgeous man in the pond.

Nate's powerful strokes cut through the water at a punishing pace. Liana wondered what demons he was trying to exorcise. She realized now that he'd spent most of his life learning to cope with pain, anger, and rejection.

She wanted to teach him how to share the burdens he carried, but it would take a lot of time to renew his faith in human nature. First, she had to prove that he could trust the love she felt for him. Then, if she was lucky, he might learn to have faith in the future.

When Nate finally slowed his pace, Liana stepped to the bank of the pond and dipped one foot into the water. The splash she made was a deliberate ploy to gain his attention, and it worked.

His brilliant eyes glinted like gems in the sunshine.

Liana could hardly breathe as those eyes roved up her bare legs, past the skimpy shorts and shirt, and over her face to wide eyes that were sparkling with emotion.

What Nate found was undisguised love and longing. It made his blood pound riotously in his head. It made his body tighten with need. It made him wary, and he planted himself in the center of the pond at a safe distance from where Liana stood.

"Good morning," she called softly to him.

Nate fought to regulate his breathing. He wondered if this was how Liana had felt when he'd interrupted her skinny-dipping. She would have been equally wary, but not half as excited. He couldn't resist taunting her.

"Are you aware that this is private property?" he demanded, his tone low and rough.

"Yes, and I know which one of us is trespassing." She didn't sound the least bit apologetic.

Her eyes never left him, and Nate felt a familiar rush of arousal. Neither the vigorous exercise nor the cool water could weaken his desire.

In the long, eventful hours since they'd made love, his fears of inadequacy had increased. He couldn't deny wanting her, but he'd decided that they shouldn't risk any further involvement. He had to make her understand.

"We need to talk," said Liana. "Our discussion in your bedroom last night was rudely interrupted."

"Not here, not now." His tone was adamant. Thoughts of her had tormented him all night. He was one big ache, and his resistance was at an all-time low.

"I think this is a perfect place," she insisted, her

eyes daring him to disagree. "This is where we first met. You seemed very interested in me that morning."

Nate frowned. "That was before . . ."

"Before what?" Liana taunted gently. "Before you realized that you could actually learn to care about the woman inside the body?"

Nate's frown deepened. He didn't like her reasoning. "Before my scandalous past caught up with me and threatened your reputation," he clipped.

"You weren't responsible for the scandal, and I don't feel threatened," she countered lightly.

Nate wanted to believe her. He knew his mother had told her the facts. Liana had come to his defense before knowing the whole truth. He would never find the words to tell her how much that meant to him, but he would do his best to see that she never suffered for her faith in him.

"This still isn't the time or place," he argued. "Go home. I'll get dressed and come over there."

Liana ignored his suggestion. "This is where we made love for the first time," she reminded huskily. "I've never felt so special in all my life, and I think it's the perfect place to discuss how we feel about each other."

Nate's body quaked at the reminder of their loving. He'd thought of little else for the past thirty-six hours. He wanted her with a desperation that was unbearable, but he knew it was wrong to take the physical gratification when he had nothing else to offer.

"Turn your back, and hand me my clothes," he told her, knowing she wasn't going to be persuaded to leave. "Then we can talk."

Liana's eyes stayed locked with his, and she

slowly shook her head. Then, without losing eye contact, she began to unfasten the buttons of her blouse.

"Liana!" Nate's tone was dark with warning. His big body trembled, and the ache in his groin intensified.

She slowly stripped off her shirt and tossed it to the boulder. Next she stepped out of her shorts. Her eyes never faltered as she reached for the hooks of her bra.

"Liana! Stop right now. We have to talk!"

Nate heard the panic in his own voice, but he felt like a drowning man. He knew he couldn't resist her for long. Not if she got too close. Not if she touched him.

The soft breeze made her nipples crest as it blew across her naked breasts. Liana added her bra to the mounting pile of discarded clothing. She'd never felt so wanton and needy. Her eyes shone with determination.

"I think you're right," she told her reluctant lover. "This isn't the time to talk."

With that, she stepped out of her panties. She stood proud, but trembling, at the edge of the pond.

Nate's mouth went dry. His eyes flared hotly. Every muscle in his body went taut. She was so exquisite and so sensually intoxicating. The sight of her made him burn, even in the water. Blood pulsed through his veins like hot lava and pumped into his groin with devastating force.

Liana hesitated only briefly before diving into the pool. Her breath caught as the cool water rushed against her heated flesh. Then she was surfacing a few feet from Nate.

He had backed against the bank where he could stand without treading water. His eyes dilated as Liana moved closer. Her hair was wet and slick against her head, enhancing the natural beauty of her features. The look in her eyes pierced his heart. She was brazen, yet vulnerable. She moved boldly toward him, yet her eyes pleaded for reassurance.

Nate shuddered in an effort to control the desire that ravaged his body. He was completely vulnerable, too. He couldn't even protect her if they made love.

"This isn't smart." He growled a hoarse warning.

Liana's eyes locked with his. Her voice was slightly unsteady, but the conviction was strong. "I love you."

She still hadn't touched him, but her words were like a physical and emotional caress. The caress was hot and sweet. Heat rocked through him.

"You're not cut out for an illicit affair," Nate insisted roughly, "and I can't offer you anything else."

"You could love me," she whispered, her eyes devouring his strong, handsome features.

"I can't marry you." He had to make her understand.

"I didn't ask," she whispered softly.

"You'll be leaving at the end of the summer. You want a life in the big city," he reminded harshly. "I'm never going to leave this farm."

He had to make the break now. If they had an affair, if he gave in to the primitive emotion raging inside him, he would never find the strength to let her go.

"I've had a change in plans," she declared as she gently balanced on her toes to tread water.

Nate's eyes narrowed. His heart rate increased painfully. "What kind of change?"

"I'm considering the job opportunities in this area," she explained quietly.

Nate's tone grew louder and more fierce. "Why? I thought you were dedicated to a career in New York."

"Priorities change."

"But dreams don't die," he warned darkly.

"They can change, too."

A tremor quaked through Nate. His breathing was growing more ragged by the minute. He had his hands balled into fists to keep from reaching for her. He wanted to believe she loved him enough to alter her career plans, but he didn't think she could do it without regret.

"I don't want you to ever feel cheated," he rasped, managing to voice his greatest fears. "I don't want your reputation destroyed by association with me, and I don't want you to end up hating me."

Liana let the gentle lapping of the water shift her closer to Nate. She splayed her hands on his chest and relished the feel of his hard, slick flesh. Her fingers played with the soft, swirling hair, but she didn't touch him anywhere else.

Nate closed his eyes and savored the feel of her hands on his body. She was killing him by inches. When her nails gently raked his nipples, he moaned deep in his chest. His stomach muscles quivered.

"Touch me, Nate," Liana coaxed huskily. "Hold me in your arms. Kiss me until I can't breathe."

Nate's response was another agonized groan. How

could any man be expected to resist such temptation from the woman he loved? How could he not love her?

His arms enfolded her and pulled her tightly against him. A tortured moan escaped him as her soft, sleek body pressed against his hard, aching form. Her nipples brushed his chest. He felt them grow more rigid, and every muscle and nerve in his body quivered in reaction.

Liana's hands slid over his shoulders and up his neck. Her fingers sunk into the thick waves of his hair, and she tugged his head closer. When their mouths finally met, it was like striking a match to a fuse. Both their bodies exploded with desire. Passion raged, hot and heavy, between them.

Liana plunged her tongue between his teeth, sampling and savoring every inch of his mouth. He sucked greedily at her sweetness, and erotic sounds of satisfaction rumbled from one to the other. When she finally withdrew her tongue, he filled her mouth with his while she suckled hungrily.

Nate found firm footing in more shallow water. His hands stroked and kneaded the tender flesh of her backside until his need grew too urgent to control. He grasped her hips and ground her body against the throbbing hardness of his loins.

Liana dragged her mouth from his and gasped for breath. Nate's lips slid down her throat to her breasts. He pressed her backward until he could capture a diamond-hard nipple between his teeth. The gentle torture made Liana cry out in excitement.

He gave each nipple equal attention; first nipping, then licking, and finally sucking until she was grinding her hips against his in a feverish demand.

Liana's fingers clenched and unclenched in the thickness of his hair. "Nate!" she cried as the fires in her body kept growing hotter and hotter. His mouth was igniting flames of desire that blazed a trail from her nipples to her womb.

"Nate, please!" She was almost sobbing now. When he finally lifted his head, she slammed her mouth against his for another long, deep, ravenous kiss.

He slid one big hand between their slippery bodies until he found the heart of her desire, then swallowed her passionate moans while stroking her intimately.

Liana threw her head back, trembled like a leaf, and then begged. "Please, Nate, please. I want you so bad!"

"I can't protect you," he protested thickly. He didn't trust his control enough to consider pulling back at the last minute.

"I don't care, Nate. I need you so much," she cried huskily. Her passion-darkened eyes locked with his. "If you love me, I'm not afraid of anything."

"Even a baby?" he rasped.

In response to his question, Liana locked her mouth with his. Her tongue plunged deep. She wrapped her legs around his hips and offered herself to him. Nate's breath spilled out in an agonized rush.

"Be sure, Liana! God, be sure! I'll never let a child of mine be called a bastard. If you let me love you again, you're mine, and I'll never let you go." His tone was raw as he tried give her one last warning. "I don't have enough strength to let you go again!"

In response, she pressed closer, and his moan of pleasure was low and primitive. His broad hands guided her until their bodies were locked. Then they both went very still, enjoying the exquisite pleasure of the intimacy.

"It feels so good!" Liana whispered huskily, and buried her face against his neck.

"So good," he muttered thickly. His lips found the tender skin of her throat. "I wish I could keep you this close forever."

"Forever?" Liana challenged on a broken sigh. "I'm yours forever, or however long you want me."

Nate's brutal control snapped. Her unconditional offering of love made a mockery of his doubts. His hands locked on her thighs, and he held her tightly as he drove them to unscaled heights. He wasn't easily sated, and he made sure Liana's body was rippling with satisfaction before he found his own fulfillment.

When his knees buckled, Nate relaxed against the bank and clutched Liana tightly against him. Water continued to lap over their bodies, but they didn't mind. Neither of them wanted to be parted for even a minute.

Nate slid one hand into the silken hair at her nape and gentle massaged the back of her head. When his breathing had regulated somewhat, he spoke to her.

"I love you," he declared hoarsely.

Liana moaned softly and kissed his neck.

"I've never said that to anyone else in my whole life," he admitted gruffly, "not even to my mother. There were times when I wished I could say the words, but I could never get them past my throat. They come easy with you."

"I hope that means your love for me is special," she whispered against his ear. "Because my love for you is the most wonderful thing that's ever happened to me.''

Nate planted swift, hard kisses all over her face. He tilted her head until their eyes were level. ''Will you marry me?'' he asked.

Liana's eyes darkened with emotion, ''Not unless you're absolutely sure that's what you want.''

''Is it what you want?''

''Yes.''

The strength of her reply brought a grin to Nate's lips. ''It's what I want, too, but I was afraid to believe.''

''I'll make a believer out of you,'' Liana promised him. ''As long as you love me as much as I love you.''

''I love you more.''

''No way,'' she argued and stole a kiss.

Nate enveloped her in his arms again. With a little shifting, he managed to get them both out of the water and to a soft blanket of clover. He kept Liana on top of him and tenderly stroked her satin-smooth flesh. The sun bathed their damp bodies with shimmering warmth.

''I have an old business associate who just bought a chain of motels in central Ohio,'' Nate told her as he continued to caress her lovingly.

''He's looking for someone who could take the nondescript and make each one unique. I told him about this really talented decorator I know.''

Liana finally stirred. She was touched by his genuine concern and respect for her career, but she didn't want to talk about her work.

Propping her elbows on his chest, she lifted her head to look directly at him. She loved the sexy glimmer and shimmering brilliance in his beautiful eyes. She'd never known anyone with eyes like his that sparkled in amorous invitation. They mesmerized her, and lavished her with sensual warmth.

"Did anyone ever tell you, you have bedroom eyes?" she asked as she cupped his face in her hands.

"Bedroom eyes?" he queried. The sensual message in hers was making him hot again.

Liana nodded. "Eyes that make a woman think of satin sheets, silk underwear, and hours of erotic pleasure," she explained as she gently ground her hips into his.

Nate's eyes darkened. She obviously didn't want to discuss her career. He felt the familiar cadence of blood pumping heavily through his veins. He felt Liana's nipples harden against his chest, and knew she felt his reaction to her seductive flattery. He dipped his head and brushed kisses across the baby-soft skin of her breasts.

"Maybe you'd better make sure no other woman gets the same ideas about me," he suggested roughly.

"How?"

"Promise to marry me and love me forever."

Liana's response was husky, but firm with conviction. "I promise. I promise. I promise."

Their mouths met, their tongues warm, and wet, and seeking. They silently pledged their love with bodies, hearts, and souls that vowed to honor the same commitment.

EPILOGUE

Liana felt a thrill of pride each time she stepped through the door of her new home—the home she shared with Nate. February had been a cold month, but the worst of the winter weather was behind them now, and she happily shed her heavy coat, boots, and gloves in the entrance hall.

The chill of winter was quickly driven away as she stepped further into the inviting warmth of the house. What had once seemed like a mausoleum was now filled with life, love, and laughter. Every room was a unique blend of old and new. The decor was bright, the ambiance welcoming.

They'd been married for more than six months, yet she felt a bride's excitement every time she came home from work. Nate was usually waiting for her, and she was always wild to see him. She missed him anytime they were apart.

"Nate!" Liana shouted so that she could be heard throughout the house. "I'm home!"

She continued with the career she loved because her husband had invited hundreds of people to his house to show off her decorating skills. He continually bragged about her talent. Now she had an office at home and enough business to keep her as busy as she wanted to be.

Nate still didn't want her to work for too many hours a day. He insisted he worried about her health, but she knew he wanted her with him as much as she wanted to be with him.

"Hey, Harden, are you here?" she called while walking down the hall toward the back of the house.

Liana found her husband with one shoulder propped against the door of their family room. His jeans-clad legs were crossed at the ankle, and his arms were crossed over his chest. The gleam in his eyes was predatory as he watched her approach.

"You looking for me, little lady?" Nate queried in a deep, sexy drawl.

The sight of him always made Liana's pulse race. The come-hither look in his eyes made her insides melt and her knees go weak. Her body had become very accustomed to his incredibly generous style of loving.

She slowly stepped in front of Nate, standing toe to toe, yet not quite touching. "Are you the man of the house?" she inquired huskily.

"Who wants to know?" he asked arrogantly.

"The woman of the house."

"What do you want with the man of the house?"

"I have something for him."

Nate's eyes darkened. "Is he gonna like it?"

Liana's smile widened with sensual promise. "He's gonna love it."

Nate straightened from his nonchalant position, but he still didn't touch her. "How do you know he'll love it?"

"He always loves my kisses," she insisted, reaching up to cup his face.

"Kisses?" Nate growled low in his throat. "You have kisses for the man of the house?"

"Bunches of 'em," Liana teased as she brushed her lips over his.

"Mmm . . . bunches," Nate mumbled his approval as his lips settled more firmly over hers.

They took their time saying hello. Even though they'd been parted only a few hours, they never seemed to get enough of each other. Their tongues tangled, teased, and tasted.

Nate's hands slipped through the front of her suit jacket to grasp her waist. Her blouse was silk. He loved the feel of the fabric and the warmth of her skin beneath it. His fingers tightened and he pulled her closer. His mouth grew more demanding, and Liana quickly met the demand with a hungry moan.

The next instant, she was being swept into his arms and carried to his favorite easy chair. Nate sat down and eased her onto his lap. Liana clung to him, trusting him completely, never bothering to lift her mouth from his.

When their mouths finally parted for air, he alternately nibbled at her lips and complained about her absence. "I missed you. I always miss you. You were gone too long."

"I missed you, too," Liana murmured against his mouth. She had been gone a couple of extra hours today, but she had a feeling her grumbling husband wouldn't mind once he found out where she'd spent the time.

He helped her slip her jacket off her shoulders and let it drop to the floor. Then he wrapped one arm around her shoulders to tuck her close to his chest. With the other hand, he began an adoring caress of the womanly shape beneath the silk.

"Mmm . . ." Liana moaned her approval of the big hand cupping her breast. She let her lips slide from his mouth, down his chin, to the open collar of his shirt. There she pressed a wet kiss against the strong column of his throat.

"What did you think of the new hotel you visited today?" Nate asked in an interested, but slightly pre-occupied tone. He was busy concentrating on her body's responsiveness to his touch.

Liana unfastened a few more buttons of his shirt and continued her exploration of his chest. "It's going to need a lot of work, but there's no hurry, so I'll be able to take my time with the whole project."

"Good." Nate wanted her to be happy about her work, but he also wanted her with him as much as possible.

"How was your day?" Liana asked while her tongue played with the tight, curling hairs she'd un-covered. "Anything exciting happen while I was gone?"

Nate's hand stilled for just an instant, and he grew a little tense. He immediately relaxed and resumed his caresses, but not before Liana had noted the tension in him.

She drew back in his arms and looked directly into his eyes. "Did something happen?" she asked in a concerned tone. "It's not your mother, is it?"

Liana had become really fond of her mother-in-law. Olive and Peter still traveled extensively, but they made their home with the newlyweds whenever they wanted to settle down for a little while.

"Mom's fine," Nate assured her. "She called from Paris and said they'd be home at the end of next week."

Liana didn't like the way he was avoiding her eyes, nor his deliberate attempt to distract her by slipping his hand inside her blouse.

"Nate?" she queried, framing his face with her hands and forcing him to look at her. "What else happened today?"

His handsome features hardened, and anger glinted in his eyes. "I got a check in the mail."

Liana's brows rose. "That upset you?"

He made a move to shift her out of his arms, but Liana refused to budge. She tightened her grip on his head. "Who was the check from, and what's it for?"

Nate's eyes narrowed. "The legal hassle over this house has finally been settled," he growled. He still couldn't bring himself to call Drenasis his grandfather. He couldn't even say the dead man's name.

"I got a check for the full amount I paid for this place, plus my half of the inheritance."

"That is terrible!" she scoffed, tongue in cheek. She wanted to tease the tension out of him. "You're mad because you're several hundred thousand dollars richer?"

Her ploy earned her a glare and grunt of impatience.

"You know I've never wanted anything from him. I bought this place with my own money, and I didn't want a refund. I don't want an inheritance from a man who didn't have the decency to accept my existence while he was alive.''

Liana sighed and rested her head on his chest. She slipped her arms around him and hugged tightly, hating the reaction Nate always had to any mention of his inheritance.

''I wish you could accept the money and stop dwelling on the past,'' she told him quietly. In response, she felt him grow stiffer with anger and resentment.

''You think I should just forgive and forget?'' he demanded tightly.

Liana sat up and locked her eyes with his. ''No, I don't expect you to do that. I'm never going to forgive or forget the injustice of how you were raised,'' she declared with passionate intensity. ''But I had hoped . . .''

The courage to complete her thought deserted her, and she shifted her eyes from the intensity of his. She was very secure in Nate's love, but still shy about discussing her most private hopes and dreams. He encouraged her to tell him everything, yet she knew he suffered from a lot of emotional baggage that he wouldn't share with her.

When she tried to move off his lap, a shiver of fear rippled through Nate. He couldn't bear even the slightest sign of rejection from Liana. He lived with the constant fear that she would grow tired of him and realize she'd made a mistake by marrying him. No amount of loving seemed to lessen the insecurity.

His arms tightened around her possessively. When she laid her head back against his arm, he reached out to stroke the satin softness of her hair. "Tell me," he coaxed softly. "What did you hope?"

Liana felt a blush of shyness warm her cheeks, but she wanted to explain. Her eyes locked with his again. "I know we haven't been married long compared to people who have lived together for forty or fifty years," she began.

"But I want to give you so much love that you don't have any room left in your heart for anger and bitterness. I want my love to be strong enough to heal all the old wounds," she ended on a husky whisper.

Her words created a tight ache in Nate's chest. God, how he loved her! More than words could ever express. More than life itself. He crushed her against his chest and buried his face in her hair as tremors of emotion coursed over him.

"Maybe I'm just spoiled and selfish," Liana murmured against his ear, "but I want to be the most important thing in your life. I can't bear it when you're hurt by the past."

Nate's breathing was rough as he fought for control. He'd never met anyone who could tear him apart with just a word or a touch. Sometimes the strength of his love for Liana scared the hell out of him. It was still too hard for him to express the depth of his feelings in words, but there were three that came easily to him now.

"I love you," he ground out roughly, then pressed a hard kiss on the smooth flesh of her neck. "You're already the most important thing in my life," he swore in a low tone. "Don't ever doubt it."

Liana snuggled closer to the heat of his big body. She'd felt the tremors of reaction to her words. It was hard for Nate to communicate verbally, but his body language told her what she needed to know. Maybe her love and care would eventually ease the pain of his past.

There was something else she wanted to share with him, but she did so while her face was still pressed against his chest. "I made a special stop today," she told him. "That's the reason I was a little late."

Nate's voice was still gruff with emotion. "Where did you stop?" he asked.

"I went to see Dr. Martin."

Her answer caused immediate alarm. He lifted her face so that he could see her eyes. "Who's Dr. Martin?"

"My gynecologist."

"Something's wrong?" he rasped.

"Nothing that can't be fixed in about seven and a half months," Liana teased gently.

Nate relaxed because her eyes were sparkling with happiness. It took a couple of seconds for her words to make sense to him. Then his eyes widened in shock.

"You're pregnant?"

Liana nodded and gave him a brilliant smile. "We're going to have a baby."

"A baby," Nate repeated in a dazed fashion. "We're going to have a baby?"

Liana laughed delightedly. "It was bound to happen, you know. It shouldn't be such a shock. We haven't done a thing to prevent it."

Nate turned her in his arms and splayed a hand across her abdomen. His expression was awed. "A baby."

He hadn't thought it was possible to be happier

than marriage to Liana had made him. Now they were going to have a child. Maybe a little girl with silver hair and blue eyes like her gorgeous mother. Maybe a son.

The thought brought a frown to his face. Liana saw it and didn't like it. "What's wrong? Are you already worrying about how fat and ugly your wife is going to get?"

Nate gave her a long, deep kiss, holding her close to his heart. "I'd love you if you weighed three hundred pounds and had a face like a horse," he swore softly.

Liana didn't laugh at his words. She knew they were true. Sometimes she felt humbled by the purity of his love. They'd vowed to love each other for better or for worse. She prayed she would never make Nate regret his faith in her.

"Are you happy about the baby," she asked, "or does the idea of being a father bother you?"

"I'm happy." He assured her with a fierce hug and another long kiss. He badly wanted Liana to have his baby. The thought made his heart swell with pride and joy. What concerned him was the poor role-model Buford Harden had been.

"Really happy?" Liana demanded when she could catch her breath again. She sensed that something was bothering him and dampening his enthusiasm.

"I'm really happy," Nate insisted. "I just hope I can learn to be a good father. I don't want history repeating itself."

Liana got really angry and grasped his face in a firm grip, demanding his full attention. "Don't you dare compare yourself to that swine of a stepfather!"

she growled. "You don't ever have to worry about being abusive!"

Nate's expression was grim. "You can't be sure."

"I am sure!" she argued hotly. "You are so special. What do I have to do to convince you how much I love you? How can I prove my faith in you? What can I do to make you have some faith in yourself?"

Nate studied her fierce expression and flashing eyes. She was going to have his baby. She was an intelligent, caring person. The fact that she was willing to have his child was evidence that she loved and trusted him. If she harbored secret doubts about his character, she wouldn't be giving him a child.

"Nate?" Liana wanted him to tell her what he was thinking.

He grasped both of her hands and carried them to his mouth for kisses. Then he resettled her in his lap. Her silk blouse fell open to expose a lacy camisole. Nate gently slid the straps of it and her bra off her shoulders, baring her beautiful breasts.

Liana's breath caught in her throat as he leaned down to shower her sensitive flesh with warm, wet kisses.

"Nate?" Her demand was husky. "You didn't answer my question."

His bedroom eyes were dark with desire as they met hers. "You can convince me by loving me and having my baby," he told her in a deep, rough tone. "We can put that check in a trust fund for all our babies."

Liana's eyes sparkled with tears. Her smile was wide and warm. "Loving you is so easy," she whispered through a throat thick with emotion. "The baby is a gift from God. He knows our love is special. So do I.''

The words were barely out of her mouth before Nate captured it and stole one hungry kiss after another. His arms cradled her gently, but firmly, against his chest. It was a long time later before he carried her to bed.

SHARE THE FUN . . .
SHARE YOUR NEW-FOUND TREASURE!!

You don't want to let your new books out of your sight?
That's okay. Your friends can get their own. Order below.

No. 50 RENEGADE TEXAN by Becky Barker
Rane lives only for himself—that is, until he meets Tamara.

No. 57 BACK IN HIS ARMS by Becky Barker
Fate takes over when Tara shows up on Rand's doorstep again.

No. 79 SASSY LADY by Becky Barker
No matter how hard he tries, Curt can't seem to get away from Maggie.

No. 114 IMPOSSIBLE MATCH by Becky Barker
As Tyler falls in love with Chantel, it gets harder to keep his secret.

No. 141 BEDROOM EYES by Becky Barker
Nate solves Liana's dilemma but he causes a whole new set of problems.

No. 109 HONOR'S PROMISE by Sharon Sala
Once Honor gave her word to Trace, there would be no turning back.

No. 110 BEGINNINGS by Laura Phillips
Abby had her future completely mapped out—until Matt showed up.

No. 111 CALIFORNIA MAN by Carole Dean
Quinn had the Midas touch in business but Emily was another story.

No. 112 MAD HATTER by Georgia Helm
Sara returns home and is about to make a deal with the man called Devil!

No. 113 I'LL BE HOME by Judy Christenberry
It's the holidays and Lisa and Ryan exchange the greatest gift of all.

No. 115 IRON AND LACE by Nadine Miller
Shayna was not about to give an inch where Joshua was concerned!

No. 116 IVORY LIES by Carol Cail
April makes Semi a very unusual proposition and it backfires on them.

No. 117 HOT COPY by Rachel Vincer
Surely Kate was over her teenage crush on superstar Myles Hunter!

No. 118 HOME FIRES by Dixie DuBois
Leara ran from Garreth once, but he vowed she wouldn't this time.

No. 119 A FAMILY AFFAIR by Denise Richards
Eric had never met a woman like Marla . . . but he loves a good chase.

No. 120 HEART WAVES by Gloria Alvarez
Cass was intrigued by Peyton, one of the few who dared stand up to him.

No. 121 ONE TOUGH COOKIE by Carole Dean
Taylor Monroe was the type of man Willy had spent a lifetime avoiding.

No. 122 ANGEL IN DISGUISE by Ann Wiley
Sunny was surprised to encounter the man who still haunted her dreams.

No. 123 LIES AND SHADOWS by Pam Hart
Gabe certainly did not fit Victoria's image of the perfect nanny!

No. 124 NO COMPETITION by Marilyn Campbell
Case owed Joey Thornton a favor and now she came to collect his debt.

No. 125 COMMON GROUND by Jeane Gilbert-Lewis
Blaise was only one of her customers but Les just couldn't forget him.

No. 126 BITS AND PIECES by Merline Lovelace
Jake expected an engineering whiz . . . but he didn't expect Maura!

No. 127 FOREVER JOY by Lacey Dancer
Joy was a riddle and Slater was determined to unravel her mystery.

No. 128 LADY IN BLACK by Christina Dodd
The cool facade Margaret worked at so hard, melted under Reid's touch.

Meteor Publishing Corporation
Dept. 493, P. O. Box 41820, Philadelphia, PA 19101-9828

Please send the books I've indicated below. Check or money order (U.S. Dollars only)—no cash, stamps or C.O.D.s (PA residents, add 6% sales tax). I am enclosing $2.95 plus 75¢ handling fee for *each* book ordered.

Total Amount Enclosed: $_____.

____ No. 50	____ No. 110	____ No. 117	____ No. 123
____ No. 57	____ No. 111	____ No. 118	____ No. 124
____ No. 79	____ No. 112	____ No. 119	____ No. 125
____ No. 114	____ No. 113	____ No. 120	____ No. 126
____ No. 141	____ No. 115	____ No. 121	____ No. 127
____ No. 109	____ No. 116	____ No. 122	____ No. 128

Please Print:
Name _____
Address _____ Apt. No. _____
City/State _____ Zip _____

Allow four to six weeks for delivery. Quantities limited.